Wayside

Contents

Foreword

What does it take to write and publish short stories?

1. Paper and pen / typewriter / computer
2. Words
3. Sentences
4. Time
5. Patience
6. More time
7. Lots of patience

The three of us first met at a short story course in 2021. By the end we had formed a rebellion and hatched a plan to meet regularly because - why not? There were varied incentives - the dream of bestsellers, Netflix, sorry strike that - Amazon deals - or hey, just another WhatsApp group that you read periodically and then doom scroll through the messages wishing you'd reacted a month ago. But we did have one thing in common - we loved to write. The experience of writing. The moment you sit down, put pen to paper, or press those keys and step into someone's shoes - nothing beats that. Well, maybe an ultra-high-tech device that you plug into your nervous system, and you literally embody your character, any character. Imagine that. But until then, we choose writing.

We met online and began our first ever workshop, with a really organised agenda, taking a cue from our writing class - reading our stories together, critiquing but being nice and positive. And then, suddenly, before we knew what was happening, we let our hair down (together we have kilos of hair, evenly distributed) and talked about books we love to read, the ones we disliked, the ones we abhorred, characters we loved, our doubts, fears, someone's dog or cat, bizarre and annoying neighbours, accidents that happened to us, trauma, accidents waiting to happen, lice, ticks, the weather, always the weather, blankets, travel and sometimes but to be fair, not that often, we would graze politics (how can you not? Have you seen the world we live in?) and every so often one of us would provide prompts, inspire us and we would write together, for short bursts, read what we'd written, and sign off until next time. At some point we decided we should publish our work because – why not? One of us took the lead, pushed us to edit, to re-edit and did all the back-office work you're holding in your hand, or staring at on your screen.

So, what does it take to write and publish short stories?

8. Good friends who inspire and support your love of writing.

Now go read.

The Well of Wayside

Janet Armstrong

Way back in the time of Queen Anne, in the waterlogged flats of the East Anglian fens, stood a lonely inn, much favoured by travelling folk - not so much for fine hospitality or exquisite fare, but for the secure passage it could assure the wandering wayfarer across the treacherous marshes. The folk living in those parts were well known for their superstitious nature, and some say rightly so, for the Fens are to this day awash with rumours of spiteful witches, rabid hellhounds, and fornicating devil-worshippers.

And therein lies a tale. The Wayside Inn, a long, brick-built cottage with a low-slung reed roof, a damp earthen floor and a low, beamed ceiling that bowed in the middle, occupied an isolated position aside a rough strip of road leading across the flattest, most waterlogged, and most treacherous stretch of the Eastern Marshes. The safest route through the marshes was by wherry or skiff through the backwater channels, but there were those who preferred to brave the mire by land - on foot, by cart, or on horseback.

Old Sarah Wright had kept the inn going with her sister Mary since the death of her husband Jeremiah many years before. No one knew of any children; some said they had moved up to the city years before; others spoke of infants who had never matured beyond their fifth year - it was nothing out of the ordinary in those days; the isolation, chronic disease and harsh winters made certain of such things.

Sarah and Mary's age meant that they couldn't offer the best hospitality; the service was slow and forgetful, the soup nearly always cold and the bread often hard and stale, but that aside, Wayside Inn was the perfect stop for passing wayfarers, for at the side of the inn was an ancient well, from which the lady innkeepers drew water each day. The well was a useful source of water for the ladies, as the steady throughput of guests required an equally steady supply of strong cottage ale. But this was not the sole purpose of the well, as the superstitious folk of the Fens stubbornly maintained that a gift for the well from each passing traveller would ensure safe passage for all those who ventured across the marshland. Wayfarers could ignore this, not just at their own peril, but at the peril of all who sought secure deliverance to the other side of the swamp, for they would arouse the anger of the Whistling Wench.

Turning a blind eye to the vagaries of the Whistling Wench would surely bring ill fortune upon any man, woman or child who chose to do so, and blight all fellow travellers for the entire length of their journey. A gift, or token, however small, for the well at the inn would indulge the wench, quell her wrath, and ward off any ungodly misdemeanours, thereby ensuring safe passage for the traveller and their companions. Visitors would cast a silver penny, or a small piece of jewellery, or some other lucky charm into the black mouth of the well before putting their horses in harness, saddling up, and setting off onto the windswept marsh side road, and this would guarantee them safety until they reached the port of Yarmouth at the other side.

Old Sarah and Mary could not remember how long this ritual had subsisted at the inn. They only knew that their parents had performed it, and their parents before them. Theirs was not to question why, theirs was simply to remind each traveller of their need to make an offering to the well before making their farewells. But on occasions there would be an objection by those who

8

considered themselves above such things, or from those who hailed from beyond the flat lands and maintained a proud ignorance of the local folklore and its superstitions.

And so, one January morning a thick mist descended upon the fields in the night, accompanied by an evil wind with a bite as sharp as rats' teeth. A wealthy squire from Essex and his servant boy had taken lodgings for the night at Wayside and had given Sarah and Mary a thumping sore head with their complaining and plain bad manners. The squire had complained of lice in his bed and wanted a change of room, the servant had claimed access to Sarah's old Dutch oven to cook his master's breakfast, being rudely dismissive of the old lady's own kitchen skills, and the squire's ill-mannered horse had kicked the stable door to pieces. When it came for Sarah to remind them of their duty to indulge the Whistling Wench, the arrogant squire dismissed her words of warning with a nonchalant flick of the hand, saddled his disobedient mare and cantered away into the fog, followed by his servant boy running behind on foot.

The pair had not ventured far when the mare's ears pricked, and her pace quickened. Sensing something was not right with the animal, the squire pulled hard on the reins and brought her to a walk as he cocked his head to one side and listened intently. His ears glowed crimson red with the cold and a gale blasted across the flats like a cannon, but sure enough, he could still make out a soft, melodic piping from the deep watery ditch that ran along the road. This was not the whistle of the wind; the piping was more delicate, tuneful, and enchanting, like nothing he had heard before. The notes wrapped themselves around him like a silken scarf and lulled his senses into dull submission. He dismounted and, without a word handed the reins of the mare to his servant boy. His ears following the sweet melody of the pipes, the squire thrust his heavy feet through the fog into the reed beds until the water lapped around his boots. The notes seemed to float across the cold frosty water, toying playfully with his ears, stroking him and caressing him into a torpor. Through the thickening fog, he could just barely make out the pale, wraith-like shadow of a girl clothed only in loose, light garments. She glided, dancing between the reed blades, waving in the wind like a willow, luring and beguiling him into a hopeless trance. Oblivious, he acquiesced, and stepped deeper into the dyke, seduced by the sensual melody, cracking the icy shards upon the water's surface one by one, surrendering to the charm, until the water finally took him and bathed him like a sleeping baby in its cold arms. In a second, he was gone, engulfed by the marsh, and the ice cast its frigid limbs back over the channel. The wench was duly compensated, fully fed and content, ready to sleep again until the next feast.

Troubled by his master's absence and the horse's agitation, the servant took it upon himself to mount the saddle and control the beast, but his handling skills lacked. The bit in the animal's mouth was savage, and each tug on the reins riled her until she sought revenge on the boy by bucking her powerful hindlegs, rearing a thick, muscular neck and throwing him off her back onto the frozen road. The fall knocked him cold, and the disburdened mare galloped back to the inn, astute enough to know where a warm stable and a fresh manger of hay would await her.

It wasn't long before the boy was found and brought back to Wayside where the sisters provided him with a warm bed and some

10

of their finest home brewed tonic. He came to his senses just long enough to murmur a few words about unearthly piping sounds emanating from the fog before he lost consciousness for the final time. The bloated body of the squire was recovered downstream a few months later, held together only by its thick winter clothing.

The winter had provided the wench with a banquet, and the sisters shouldered her latest conquests as they shouldered everything; they pursued their everyday tasks with the same determination, despite ever-growing aches and pains, and passers-by continued to frequent the inn and indulge the well with coins and charms. But the wench would grow hungry, and despite the best efforts of the sisters to thwart her worst intentions, there was an inevitability that sooner or later, a hapless wayfarer would meet a damp end in her diaphanous arms.

The day came in the autumn when the days grew shorter and the nights longer. The wench grew impatient; the ladies had been assiduous in ensuring that summer visitors pay reverence to the well, but it was time, and time came in the form of a ropemaker from Boston. Isaac Waldron had trade to attend to in Yarmouth and had brought samples of his wares carefully tucked away in neat bundles in his cart, which was pulled in harness by a solid pair of black and white cobs. Isaac prided himself on both his workmanship and horsemanship; his thriving business had been built from his own hard graft and sweat, and he deserved the financial returns that came as a result. Isaac was a practical fellow, who called a spade a spade; he had no time for fripperies, fancy curios or false beliefs.

Isaac spent a comfortable night at the inn, ate Sarah's plain food heartily and without complaint, helped the ladies to move half a dozen heavy wooden hogsheads, skipped out the horses' stables, leaving them spotless, and even climbed on the rickety old roof of the cottage to batten down some loose reeds blown out of place by high winds. Sarah and Mary, appreciative of his help and indebted for his kindness, sought to ensure his protection from the wench by entreating him to indulge the well, but Isaac, being a hands-on, no-nonsense type, refused, replying that he had no need for such stuff and nonsense. Old Sarah was beside herself, for she had taken fondly to the fellow for his kindness and tugged at his coattails as he climbed into the driving seat of his cart, clicked his tongue at the cobs, flicked the whip, and trotted away.

Isaac's journey progressed well, as he was a competent horseman and had made many such business journeys across the eastern side of the country, stopping at inns along the way. He enjoyed the fresh air and the company of passers-by, who he often asked to join him on his journey, as travelling in those days was a lonely process. On this day, he met no such travellers and became bored with the lack of company. Imagine therefore his delight when he heard a charming pipe melody drifting from the willows along the edge of the marshes.

Pulling the horses to a halt, Isaac dismounted from the driving seat of his cart and called out to the piper. But no reply came and no amount of calling, and hallooing could draw any response. Still, the music continued, and Isaac grew curious. Pushing his way through the line of willows fringing the water, he made out the cloudlike silhouette of a wisp of a girl, holding a silvery flute, from which came the sweetest of songs, warming his kind heart with its soft melody. Enchanted by the waterside concert the girl performed so tenderly,

12

Isaac fetched the cold mutton and eggs prepared for him by Sarah and Mary and searched for a dry spot along the bank so he could sit and enjoy the music.

It seemed to him the perfect spot for luncheon. He waved at the girl across the water, and she returned the gesture, still playing sweetly. She drew closer to the bank, revealing the dark outline of her pitch-black eyes against an almost translucent skin. Still piping, she seemed to drift into the water deeper and deeper until the ripples at the surface shimmered and danced around her tiny waist. Alarmed, Isaac flung his jacket and boots into a shrub and dived headlong into the culvert, thrashing his arms and legs in a bid to reach the poor creature, cradle her in his arms, and rescue her from catching her death of cold. Few visitors are aware of the powerful undercurrents that belie the many channels in the East Anglian marshland and Isaac was not one of them. A strong, muscular fellow, he fought with all his strength, but the weight of the water powering all its might against him was too strong. The heavenly music ebbed and gurgled as the river took him under, filling his lungs with watery song and piloting him gently to a forever sleep among the weeds on the bed of the channel. The wench had sung for her supper and for now would rest until her craving for human flesh was roused once more.

Isaac possessed a large family who, upon hearing of the circumstances of his demise, swore vengeance upon the disingenuous spirit that had dragged him to a premature death. They travelled the long, flat roads around the Wash from the Boston ropewalk to the East Anglian marshes, through villages and towns, across fields and meadows, avowing to give Isaac the farewell he

13

deserved and to silence the wench forever. Among their number was Isaac's brother, a prominent Methodist preacher by the name of Elias, and his brood of five small children, together with Isaac's own four children and his wife, Alice. Naturally, the family took lodgings at the Wayside Inn, where the two landladies recounted the full details of Isaac's last night, pouring heavy praise upon his generosity and kindness towards them, but still passing stern remonstrance upon him for scorning the well and tempting death.

Being a man of the cloth, and having quite a reputation as a man who dealt very firmly with unnatural things, Elias assured her that no spirit, no matter how iniquitous or black-hearted, would get the better of him, and that he would vow to rid the fenland of the evil spirit that had plagued it for so long. God would be at his side and would guide him in his endeavours to deliver the local folk of the wench, once, at last, and forever.

The next morning, Elias presided over Isaac's burial at the village church and his remains were committed to God's ground, resting in peace for eternity in the care of the Lord. The family wept together, and a solemn wake was held for the deceased at the inn, where Elias recited more prayers and announced his intention to set off that night to the dyke, to raise the wench from the water and confront her with the full intensity of God's wrath.

Night had fallen. Bible and cross in hand, Elias, his family and the sisters set off in a large hay wagon across the marshes to the dyke. Elias had refused to indulge the well, either on his own behalf or that of his family. Sarah and Mary, subjugated by suspicion, as was always the way in East Anglia, lit three church candles by the well side for the Holy Trinity, recited the Lord's Prayer, and lowered

14

a satin purse of silver pennies into the black shaft.

The group did not travel far before the whistling began. The children heard it first, and then the adults. A shrill melody wended its way through the night breeze and into the roadway, frolicking temptingly with the steady beat of the horses' feet. Elias stood proud and tall in the wagon and called out in his best preacher's voice for the spirit to leave them be and return to the waters. Instead of slackening, the music intensified, and the notes grew higher and shriller. Elias reiterated his command with the higher authority of God, but the notes grew louder and more tortured. He knew the wench would become more indignant and more resentful with every demand and with every mention of the Lord. Stepping down from the wagon, Elias signalled to his fellow travellers to remain seated, while he strode through the trailing willows to the water's edge, bible and crucifix in hand. The wench was waiting for him, fluting wildly, the black eyes darker and hungrier than usual and the tune ever higher and more staccato-like. But Elias was ready. Holding his bible in both hands, arms stretched out before him, he chanted furiously with all the power he could muster,

'God of Heaven, God of Earth,' he cried. 'God of the angels and the archangels: Michael, Gabriel, Uriel, Remiel. God of the holy martyrs and prophets, Almighty God who has such fearful and majestic power to bestow unto us immortal life after mortal death; for there is no other true God than thou, our Creator of Heaven and of Earth, our Lord; I humbly entreat thee to deliver this errant and evil serpent from the realm of the unclean spirits and take her unto thine gentle arms for mercy.' His whole frame shook. Pausing for a moment, he swung his head up to the heavens, eyes bulging, and breathed in deeply, wrenching the words from the pit of his lungs: 'Amen.

The wench glided into the water, still piping a bitter, savage and violent song, her eyes turning first flame red, then ice white, then coal black again and then glimmering a deep ruby red. Her head twisted and turned on its axis, her pale face contorted in agony. She drifted deeper and deeper into the water, the heat from her fury forcing the river water out into a hot, misty vapour which rose from the surface like steam from a boiling kettle. But Elias continued, raising his crucifix high above his head, his voice unnaturally high and tortured, sweat pouring from his brow into his ears, onto his cheeks and down the nape of his neck:

'We hereby purge ourselves of thee, oh hideous damned spirit!' he continued. 'Be forever gone from this earth, thou infernal and filthy spirit, whatever thou may be! Be gone from these waters. Damn thyself forever to thy own wicked master's hell!' He proceeded to recite the Lord's Prayer, spitting out the words like venom. 'Our holy and blessed father, who art in the kingdom of heaven, hallowed be thy name, thy kingdom come,' he cried. 'Oh Lord, thy will forever be done, on our good earth as it is in thy heaven of miracles. Give us our daily bread, Oh great Lord, forgive us our worst trespasses, for we forgive those who trespass against us. Lead us weak and sickly folk not into temptation but deliver us from evil. For thine is the only kingdom, the power and the glory, for ever and ever. Amen.' Then, sprinkling blessed water onto his crucifix, he cast it far out into the channel.

The Whistling Wench recoiled in horror, dropping the pipe into the dyke. Clutching her neck, she finally disappeared beneath the surface with a ghastly, inhuman scream. Gasping for air, Elias kept his bible firmly stretched out before him in his right hand, his left upon his chest. His features glowed a dark crimson, and he stood there transfixed, eyes glazed over, unable to move. But he could not relinquish his grip and when the rest of the party came searching for him, he was lying dead on the edge of the water, still firmly grasping his bible.

The funeral party drove silently and solemnly back to the inn; it would be a long night. For comfort and sympathy, the sisters brewed up a restorative remedy for their grieving guests from a combination of herbs and ale. In the steamy silence of the inn's parlour, Sarah racked her brains, for she knew what awaited; it had happened before, many years ago. The wench had taken revenge upon Elias, but superstition decreed that it was not only the errant traveller who would be avenged, but also any fellow travellers, unless they had honoured the well in the usual way. There was no folkloric panacea that she could recall, and the wench would surely return; it was simply a matter of time. But what terrified Sarah most was the children; there were nine of them. Nine: a number she recalled only too well. She stared at Mary with wide, anguished eyes and Mary returned the gaze with terror in her own tortured eyes; she remembered too. They did not need to form the words with their tongues; the memory was etched on their minds like initials on a fine man's wine glass.

It had been an evil night, one that both sisters had fought to erase from their combined memories through hard work, toil, labour and duty. That cold Christmas night, Jeremiah had led both her children and Mary's together, all nine of them, to midnight mass at the church and had neglected his duty at the well. Upon their return, they had been taken in the river's stream; the bridge they had been crossing had collapsed under them in the storm, and not a soul between them had survived. The sisters never spoke of it, and few villagers could remember it, but finally, like the prodigal son, it was back to haunt them, and they were powerless against it.

Sarah rose to her tired, unsteady feet and stepped out into the yard. Stooping in despair, shoulders hunched over the side of the well, she begged, supplicated and implored the wench to spare Isaac and Elias's children, offering herself in exchange, offering her sister in exchange, knowing that they were but poor substitutes, mutton and not lamb, scarcely enough to sate the wench's appetite.

The morning came and all was still well. The sisters silently packed the usual plain lunches for the travellers, who would return to Boston that very day, taking Elias's body with them for burial at his chapel amongst his own congregation. It was a sombre departure. The sisters wept profusely, as did the children and Isaac's wife. All of them knew the eventual outcome of their journey and, perhaps, just perhaps, the wench had heeded old Sarah's supplications, because it was quick; on the way out of the village, an errant stallion, chased by its angry owner, came galloping toward them, causing their own horses to rear, and turning the hay cart full over into the river. All of them drowned instantly, horses and all, trapped underwater by the heavy cart: nine children, Alice, their driver and the two fine-looking fell ponies who had pulled them faithfully all the way from Boston.

That Sunday, the church bells tolled solemnly and slowly eleven times for eleven dead; Elias never returned to Boston, and neither did any of his kin. To this day, they lie in the old churchyard not half a mile away from what is now known as Wayside Cottage. The summer tripper can find their names by delicately scratching away the lichen and moss from the very ancient gravestones that stand erect at the rear of the cemetery, under the shadow of the brooding yew trees that were planted long ago by the sisters to protect them from wicked spirits.

Wayside Cottage no longer has a well; it was backfilled and bricked over not long after Sarah and Mary left the place to live out their final years in the relative peace of Yarmouth town. The cottage changes hands every now and then from one owner to another; no one ever really feels at home there. Its brick walls have been painted a rosy pink, its door is bedecked with red climbing roses, and now it has a modern gas-fired range in the kitchen, a polished stone floor, and a pan tiled roof. The well is under the conservatory floor, a bright, modern room no one ever wants to sit in, for although the sun's rays provide it with a very warm and cheerful outlook, it always has a certain cold feel to it, and on blustery days, the wind whistles a queer tune through the glass roof, which some say sounds like Pan piping in the distance.

The Queue

Juliet Robinson

'Donald?'

'What?' I shook my head; my vision was clouded, and I had a sense of disconnect. I looked around; I wasn't in the hospital car park.

Seeing my confusion, the speaker gently placed her hand on my shoulder.

'It's OK Donald. You had an accident, but it's ok now.'

'What?' I stammered. I must have knocked my head. I looked at the speaker, who glowed with the flush of health that the young enjoy. She smiled kindly at me, and her mouth was filled with perfect, white teeth, the kind that paid for an orthodontist's retirement.

'You had an accident,' she repeated. Her voice was melodious. 'But it's OK now, you don't have to worry.' She smiled again, a generous smile that was all confidence. 'But I do need you to join the queue over there.'

'What?' It was hard to say, but I believe her smile wavered ever so slightly.

'I need you to join the queue over there.' She gestured and, for the first time, I became aware of my wider surroundings: a rocky mountainside that disappeared up into the clouds with an orderly queue climbing its slope. 'If you do not join the queue, you will lose your spot and we don't want that!' She laughed, a reedy, high-pitched giggle which suited her.

'What?' I asked again and her smile became fixed.

'Well Donald, those who lose their spot in the queue sometimes get misplaced and we don't want that, do we Donald?' She spoke in short, sharp bursts, enunciating every word.

'What?' I didn't mean to say what again, but I was seriously confused. My lunch break would be over soon, and I hadn't even been to the toilet. Her smile contorted, her hand fell heavily on my shoulder, and she forcibly shunted me towards the queue. Her smile was now so forced, I thought her face might crack. She guided me into place between a tall, young man and an elderly woman dressed in a bathrobe, who smiled at me.

'Jumping the queue?' She sounded amused.

I almost said, 'What?' again, but instead I shrugged and turned to my young guide. I opened my mouth and said nothing; my lips just flapped at her. I wanted to articulate my confusion, but I didn't know where to begin.

'It's OK Donald,' she said again. She sounded like my Primary Four teacher, Mrs Ryland.

'OK, it's OK! It's OK! It's OK! It's OK!' I grew shriller with every proclamation.

'That's right Donald, it's OK.' She looked pleased, glad that I finally understood.

'What's OK?' I bellowed.

She took a step back, 'Now shouting doesn't help.' She really did sound like Mrs Ryland. She even scolded me in the same singsong voice.

I bristled, I was a grown man, not a child. How dare this person speak to me like this?

22

'OK,' I snapped at her. I was tempted to shout again, but her frosty glare stopped me. The young man in front threw me a withering look.

'Look Donald,' he said sharply. 'This is the queue. We wait in the queue. We move forward when the queue moves forward, and sometimes someone comes along and slots in ahead of us, so we take a step back.' He had a smooth and educated voice, he was poised, he radiated confidence, and he had beautiful dark eyes.

'Well, that's helpful.' I clenched my jaw.

The lady behind me gently took my arm, 'Ignore Ayo, he's just upset because he doesn't think he should be here.'

'I shouldn't!' Ayo snarled. 'I had plans! I had things to do. I was going to make a difference. I needed more time; I deserved more time.' He bristled with self-assurance, but it sounded thickly laid on.

The old lady smiled softly, 'I know, it isn't fair. But there isn't a soul here who doesn't think that. Your time came Ayo.'

My eyes whipped between them, 'Time came? No, this isn't my time, I've got to get back to work. Bodies, bodies to sort and process. I need to sort those bodies; I can't leave them in the hospital! Their depending on me! Their families are. I must get them to the chapel of rest.'

Ayo and the old lady shared a significant look. I knew that look; it was one I shared with colleagues when the bereaved didn't have a handle on things. I gave that look; I wasn't the subject of that look. I turned looking for the young woman who had forced me into line, but she was nowhere to be seen.

'Where did she go?' I demanded. I determinedly didn't look at the old lady or Ayo as I peered around, knowing I wouldn't like what I saw on their faces.

'The guides always leave; they don't like being around us. We make them uncomfortable,' Ayo explained.

'She did her job, she got you safely into the queue.' I dared to look at the old lady; her face was the mask of sympathy I had known it would be.

I was torn. I wanted answers, but I also knew I didn't want to hear what they had to say. We stood in silence; they seemed to understand I needed time. The clouds receded, exposing a rocky mountainside. I had always wanted to try mountain climbing but had never found the time. I started to think that Michael and I really should have.

A movement caught my eye, and I looked up. A dark hound trotted out of the clouds. Its eyes were blood red, and it tossed its head, scenting the wind. A howl went up and more of them loped out of the gloom. Lean, long legged and muscled, they prowled forward, and a sense of dread swept through me. I grabbed the old lady's arm, my fingers sinking into her thick bathrobe. She patted my hand and made vague soothing sounds, though her eyes were fixed on the dogs. Then a human figure strode out of the clouds. Michael. The dogs settled on their haunches, surrounding him like an honour guard. He looked wonderful, he was tanned, somehow taller and he appeared younger. He was beautiful. How had I forgotten how beautiful he had been all those years ago? My heart burst.

'Donald,' he called. And suddenly I remembered how intoxicating I had found his soft Spanish accent. Warm, husky, and full of spiced promise. I had been so deeply in love with him when we first met. The high of that love washed over me and threatened to drown me.

My hand fell from the old lady's arm, and I turned towards Michael. The second I moved, both she and Ayo grabbed me, pulling me back into the queue. I slapped at their hands and tried to jostle myself free.

'Get off me! That's Michael.' A shaft of sunlight lanced through the clouds and illuminated him. He was glorious. My stomach churned, and my heart raced.

I shoved and pushed, desperate to free myself, to scramble across the barren ground that separated Michael from me. I slipped and fell to my knees, jarring them. Ignoring the pain, I tried to crawl forward. I wriggled and suddenly one of my would-be captors lost their grip. I shot forward, my face grazing the rocks.

The moment I left the queue, a feral snarl rippled through the dogs. Michael whistled and they charged forward, crossing the ground with long, fluid bounds. I gaped up at Michael, a savage grin split his face, and his eyes blazed with hunger. He had transformed, he wasn't my Michael. My heart crashed, plunging into the void of my stomach where it shattered.

Cries and screams broke out around me as the other members of the queue saw what was bearing down on them. Animal instinct took over, the primal urge to survive. I heaved myself up and scuttled backwards, limbs flailing, broken heart pounding, my eyes fixed on the hellish hounds as they raced towards me. Hands found me and dragged me to my feet and as the hounds sprung, I closed my eyes.

A thunderous crack shook the ground, and a blazing light burned my eyes, even as they cowered behind scrunched-up eyelids. I expected pain, but it didn't come.

'Well, that's the most exciting thing that's happened around here in forever,' Ayo observed. He was aiming for casual but failed miserably. His voice had a wobble to it.

I opened my eyes. The dogs were still there, silently patrolling up and down the queue, their baleful eyes fixed on me. A near invisible barrier had halted them in their tracks, you could see it sparking slightly when the dogs got to close. Michael shrugged his shoulders, laughed indifferently, and disappeared back into the clouds, whistling for his dogs, which turned and followed him.

I started to shake. I wanted to cry, but instead I started laughing. I laughed and laughed. It made no sense that I was laughing, but I couldn't stop. I stood in my place in the seemingly endless queue and laughed. The shock of waking up and finding myself here, the high of seeing Michael as he had been when I first met him. The abject horror of him setting the dogs on me. All of this was just too much, none of it made sense and the more I tried to anchor myself to an understanding the more ridiculous it all seemed.

In front of me, Ayo's broad shoulders rocked as he barked out a deep laugh. I don't know how long we brayed liked idiotic donkeys, but when we eventually stopped, I was drained.

'I've seen what happens when the hounds take people,' the old lady croaked.

'So have I,' Ayo muttered breathlessly. 'But they didn't today so that's something to celebrate.'

He turned and smiled at me. I nodded at him, not able to return his smile. I was busy building a mental block in my brain, trying to banish the image of the demonic Michael. I didn't want to process what had happened. I felt certain that it hadn't really been him but was too afraid to ask. What if I was wrong? We stood in silence, buried in our thoughts. And time passed.

Somewhere, in front of us, far out of sight something must have happened. A space opened and Ayo took two long steps forward. I wobbled after him, that was the best my legs could do. Then we went back to standing and I returned to not thinking about where I was.

As the clouds passed and the sun came and went, we moved forward, slowly climbing up the stony mountain. After a time, voices raised in song broke the silence of the queue.

'Dare I ask?'

'It's the vendors,' Ayo replied.

'They travel the queue selling things. Food, drink, clothes, and other items. The woman who used to be behind me bought a queue jump. She cashed in a vast number of credits to skip the line. I will never forget how certain she was of herself,' the old lady admired.

'She was utterly vapid. What worth did she have? She probably spent all her credits,' Ayo scorned.

'You say that, but when they scanned her soul, she had enough to pay for the queue jump. She did something to earn those credits,' the old woman replied.

'Bloody influencers,' Ayo spat. Though I didn't know what the hell they were talking about, I agreed with him; I found influencers to be shameless self-promoting fools.

'Jealousy is ugly Ayo, and it doesn't suit you,' she chided.

The singing grew louder as the vendors drew closer. They were certainly taking their time, it seemed like forever before they came into view. But when they did, they didn't disappoint. They were a spectacle, a riot of colour and movement. Dancers ranged around a large cart which was drawn by two gleaming chestnut horses. Singers sat atop the wagon and though they sang in a language I didn't understand, their songs were still hauntingly beautiful. Voices twined in intimate harmony. The procession moved slowly and stopped constantly. A tall, willowy woman would approach the customer, and sometimes she would return to the cart to collect purchased merchandise. I found myself becoming increasingly impatient.

'Have you ever bought anything?' I asked the old lady.

'No,' she replied. 'Though I am tempted by a change of clothes. I have been stuck in this bathrobe forever. Maybe some slippers.'

I glanced down at her bare feet, which were stained with mud and blue from the cold.

'You should get some shoes then,' I replied.

'It isn't that simple. You can spend credits with the vendors, but they won't tell you how many you have on account,' Ayo explained.

'That makes no sense. They're your credits, they should tell you how many you have.' I frowned as another thought crossed my mind, 'How do we earn the credits?'

'You've been earning them your whole life,' the old lady explained. 'Through your actions and deeds,' she said in a grandiose voice. Then in a quieter and slightly nervous tone, she went on. 'I am afraid I didn't do much with my life. I can't see how I would have made many credits. I didn't even have children,' she whispered.

'Children aren't the definitive marker of a successful life,' I snapped. Michael and I had been starting down that road, considering our options, looking for the best way to start our family. He had been the driving force behind it all. He had loved being part of a big, loud, and flamboyant family. I hadn't the same experience, so had been less sure that parenthood was for me, but I had hoped I might surprise myself.

'Maybe not, but to me they meant something,' she sighed. 'I was a teacher; I loved children. I always thought I would have a family, but I didn't meet Simon until it was too late.'

I didn't know what to say.

'Anyway,' Ayo eventually continued, saving us from the awkward silence. 'We all have credits; we can spend them with the vendors, or we can save them for when we get to the front of the queue.'

'What's at the front of the queue? I'm guessing it's not St Peter?' I smiled, thinking this rather witty.

'No. No saints here, just us, the vendors, the guides, the hounds and their masters.' Collectively we shuddered, and I steadied myself, trying not to think of the other Michael.

'So, what is at the end of the queue?' I prompted.

Neither of my companions had an answer for that question, they just knew we would need credits when we got there.

The vendors took their sweet time to arrive. Everyone stopped them, though few made purchases.

When they finally reached us, Ayo waved to the lady, calling her over. She glided towards him, and I was struck by how tall she was. Ayo wasn't small, but he had to peer up at her. She passed him a black handheld device that reminded me of a tablet. He took his time looking over his choices, and she patiently watched him as he browsed. In the end though, he decided against a purchase and practically jumping up and down, I waved her over.

She smiled at me as she approached, 'A new face, welcome. I hope your journey is quick and peaceful.' Her voice was crisp and clear. I looked at her and couldn't help being reminded of Norse stories about ice giants. She was huge, her skin was tinged blue, and her hair tumbled to her ankles like a waterfall of ice. I was half tempted to reach out and touch her skin, which I was sure would be chilled.

'Yes, I haven't been here long,' I confirmed, sticking my hand out eagerly for the tablet.

'You may be surprised,' she smiled, flashing sharp teeth.

I looked at her and decided I didn't want to know what she was hinting at. It was bad enough being here. Why would I want to know how long I had been trapped in this barren place? I bit my lip and

30

took the tablet from her.

As soon as I had it in my hand, the screen flashed to life, and I was looking at a typical online shopping page. My name was at the top, with my date of birth and next to it was another date. I looked up at the lady and pointed at it.

She smiled and nodded, 'Yes, you had a good run.'

'I was forty-five!' I protested. Immediately I felt foolish; it was obvious the vendor had met much younger customers.

I looked back at the tablet and selected the first tab, accessories and found myself gaping. The options were endless - Egyptian headdresses, horns, and wings to name just a few. I closed the list and selected the next one that caught my eye, companions. This list was equally extensive, there were animals and talking animal companions which were presumably pricier. My childhood pet hamster, Bumble was there. I wondered if this version of him would be less savage, Bumble had been most happy when fastened to my hand with his wicked sharp teeth. Celebrities from across the ages, notably: George Washington, Catherine the Great, Princess Diana and David Bowie. Regular people also featured, I noticed my childhood friends, some of whom I hadn't thought about in decades. My university friends and even some of my more recent work friends. Both my parents were there and my brother, Ernest.

I froze, my finger hovered over his picture, Ernest had died when I was ten. There he was, a fresh faced eight-year-old. I selected his name and the page with his details opened. I could purchase Ernest; he would accompany me in the queue and stay with me till the end. I stared at his picture; I had never gotten over losing him.

None of the items were priced. My mind raced as I tried to figure out what credit value the option shown would have.

'Can I afford everything on here?' I asked the vendor.

'You can afford the most expensive item listed. Or you could make several purchases adding up to that value.'

'What is the most expensive listing?'

'You were just considering it. Ernest, he's your top choice.'

'Would he empty my balance?'

'I am afraid I am not able to further discuss your finances.'

Ernest. There was little I wouldn't have given in life to spend five more minutes with him. I could feel their eyes on me, Ayo's and the old lady's.

'What?' I snapped. I rubbed at my eyes and threw them a don't start look.

'Donald, I know what you're thinking. I do this every time the vendors arrive. There are people on that list who I loved deeply, but I don't choose them.'

I glared at Ayo. 'And why not? You sounded so sure of your worth when we first met. You don't know me; you don't know that I haven't done remarkable things. I might have stacks of credits on my account. Don't judge me.' I shouted the last part. My words echoed around the mountainside and the vendor sucked in her lip, her eyes widening. A dog howled somewhere in the clouds and the queue shuffled closer together.

The vendor cocked her head and reached her hand out for the

tablet. I didn't move, I just stared down at the photo of Ernest. Him before cancer. Him before the treatments. Him before he faded away. He had been perfect. It should have been me, not him. He had been smart and funny. The easy-going one, whom our parents had adored.

After Ernest's death there had been a trench between my parents and me. I had helped to dig it. Their grief had been insurmountable and mine had been like fire, I didn't understand it and it consumed everything. I felt their pain as rejection. They lost him and they got to keep me. The one who never listened, who sulked, who hid away in his room, who put all his effort into avoiding them. The one who kept his life from them and pushed them away. As a child I hadn't been a bundle of hugs and joy, as a teen I had been a cauldron of seething emotion and later in life I had only anger and scorn for them. I had judged them for being small, narrow-minded people. They lived in the same village they had been born in, in the house my father's parents had left them. They travelled once a year to the Costa Brava. They voted Tory. They had been worried about immigrants and had loved Brexit. When Michael and I married they hadn't been at the top of my guest list. I had still felt their grief as rejection.

Despite the late invite they had come to our wedding. Dad had been dressed in the suit he had worn the day we laid Ernest to rest, though it no longer fitted. He had diminished. They had stood by the registry room door, unsure of their place amongst my chosen family. Then Mum had taken Dad's hand, walked him to the end of the aisle where they stood greeting our guests. Later at the party Dad had put his card behind the bar and Mum after one-to-many cab savs had drowned my new husband and I in hugs.

My eyes prickled and with considerable effort I dragged myself back into the moment. Ernest's smiling face still gazed up at me from the tablet. Yes, he should have lived, and fuck did I miss him, but I probably shouldn't have lived so much of my life wishing we could have traded places.

'Have you decided?' The vendor inquired.

I looked down at the old lady's bare feet, probably a size five.

'Yes, a pair of slippers, size five please. Make sure they are warm.' If the vendor was surprised, she didn't show it, she simply returned to the cart, where she retrieved my purchase. 'How do I pay?'

'It's automatic, the credits have been deducted from your account.'

The vendor smiled and handed me a wrapped box which I immediately passed to the old lady. Her mouth dropped open, and before she could say anything, I grunted, 'I hope they fit.'

She clutched the box briefly, but it was cold, and she was eager to dress her bare feet. Once the slippers were on, she started to thank me, but I waved her into silence. I wasn't in the mood to talk. She nodded her understanding and took the tablet from the vendor. I turned away and ignored their conversation.

We shuffled forward. New people arrived and joined the line. The hounds returned, though Michael didn't. The vendors came back along the line and this time Ayo bought a measure of whisky. Time passed, but little marked its passage. When I had long since given up hope that anything of significance would ever happen, we stumbled onto a wide plateau. Ayo, who was considerably taller than me, bounced on his tiptoes and quivered with excitement.

'I can see something up ahead!'

'What?' the old lady and I both demanded.

He started to laugh, 'An ATM machine! There's an ATM machine at the head of the queue.'

'Are you serious?' I was incredulous. No pearly gates? Not even a bar? I wanted a drink. Where were the vendors when you needed them?

'Yup, it's an ATM machine.'

The queue seemed to be moving faster now, perhaps because we could see our destination.

'Do either of you know what is going to happen?' I wanted to get out of here, but I was afraid of what might come next.

'No, but I feel like I've been here before. I just can't quite remember,' the old lady answered, her voice tinged with uncertainty.

I also had a sense of the familiar. It wasn't just because I had been here so long. Nor was it that the backdrop never changed. I just had a notion in my gut, a sense of intimacy with this place. I didn't know what was coming, but I was certain I had passed through here before.

She shuffled her feet and glanced down at her slippers. 'Do you regret buying these for me? What if you don't have enough credits for what comes next?'

She sounded tired and anxious; I could relate. I shook my head. I was worried, but I was glad I spent some of my credits on the slippers. I did, however regret not having paid to spend time with Ernest. But like my companions, I was worried about what might come next. The more credits I had saved the better.

'I shouldn't have bought the whisky,' Ayo worried.

'It's going to be fine,' I soothed.

'But I did nothing. I didn't even finish university, I dropped out three times. I was so sure I was going to be someone, but I didn't know how,' he confessed. 'I was good at sounding like I was sure of myself, that I was interesting and worthy. But I wasn't. I was insanely superficial, scratch my surface and all you would have found was a boring and selfish person.' He sunk in on himself.

'Everyone's a bit boring,' I smiled. My friends were fraying, they needed comfort, and I knew how to speak to people in this state. I slipped into work mode. In life I had been a mortician and funeral director. I prepared the bodies of the deceased, but there was more to my work. Our clients came to us raw and broken, we helped them process their grief and piece together a memorial for their loved ones.

'I was happy with my quiet life,' the old lady reflected. 'I'm sure most people would have found it dull, but it was enough for me. It would have been better with children, but what Simon and I had was good. I don't think being boring is a terrible thing.'

'I thought teachers viewed their pupils as their children. If you think about it, you had lots of children,' I offered.

'Yes, maybe I did,' she smiled, though I could tell she didn't feel that way. Clearly this was a platitude she had heard many times. She looked at Ayo, 'I don't think superficial people know they are selfish, or empty. If you'd had more time, I know you would have found yourself. Trust me, I am a teacher, and I am good at gauging a person's measure.'

If Ayo was comforted, it didn't show, his face was drawn and shadowed.

'I was too scared to try in case I failed,' he finally whispered.

I wanted to reassure him, but his words had struck a little too close to my own truth. It wasn't something I had spoken of, but it was there, nestling inside me a sense that I could and should have been more. We fell silent. The queue moved and we shuffled along. I leaned round Ayo. Only eight people remained in front of us. I flushed with anticipation. We all edged forward, closing any gaps.

Finally, it was Ayo's turn; he smiled at us, 'It has been a pleasure.'

The old lady clutched my hand, as we watched him cross the line that separated the queue from the space around the ATM. He didn't waver and he didn't look back. He reached the machine and vanished. And I was at the front of the queue. I squeezed my elderly companion's hand once, then walked forward. I almost looked back when I reached the ATM, but in that instant, I was transported away.

I found myself in the chapel of rest at work. A wicker coffin lay on the catafalque, and though its lid was closed, I knew it was mine. Light flooded through the tall, south-facing windows and the air was thick with the scent of lilies. I approached the coffin, which was simple yet elegant. Tentatively I reached out a hand to touch it, but I found I couldn't, something in me shied away. A cough drew my attention and there at the back of the room, standing by the ATM machine from the mountain was Ernest. On hesitant feet, I crossed the room to stand in front of my brother. Then he flung himself on me and I clung to him.

'How are you here?'

'Slippers,' he replied. I had forgotten his voice. I had been so sure I remembered it, but I hadn't. I burst into tears. 'You bought her slippers, so she paid for me to meet you here.'

I howled and pulled him even tighter to me, crushing him against me. Eventually I didn't have any tears left and he pushed me away and waved me forward to the ATM machine.

'You have to make a choice now,' he said.

'Can't we stay here for a bit?' I asked. 'I missed you. Mum and Dad missed you.'

'I know. I missed you guys. But I moved on and it's your turn now. It's simple, the machine will tell you the options you can afford. All you have to do is pick one.'

'And that's simple?'

'Yeah. I knew straight away.'

He took my hand and the screen flickered as cubic green text loaded onto it.

Donald (Don) Matthew Ayers, 18th of January 1967.

Fifty years forward.

Fifty years back.

Up to two hops parallel, left or right.

Cat.

'What does it mean?'

'I had more choices,' Ernest said as he peered at the screen. 'You just choose one and that's where you go to start again.'

'Like a reset? Me again, somewhere else?'

'Maybe you, maybe not, but parts of your whole.'

Still holding his hand, I studied my options. Fifty years forward, that would send me into the unknown. Fifty years back, well I had just navigated the best part of the last fifty years, so I had an idea of what to expect with that choice.

'Parallel. So, what is that? Like parallel universes?'

'Yup.'

I looked down at Ernest, I was the grown up here, yet I wanted him to provide me with answers. 'Small differences? Big differences?' I probed.

'I don't know.'

'I guess the further you go the bigger the differences?' I exhaled heavily. I was tired and this wasn't exactly what I had expected. 'Can you tell me what you chose?'

'I can't.'

'Did you have cat as an option?'

'Cat, eagle and orca, but I didn't pick an animal.'

'How do animals earn credits?' I wondered. I had a feeling that picking an animal was end game, perhaps a choice for tired souls who'd had enough. Despite my fatigue I wasn't ready for that yet.

Parallel, what was the worst that could happen with that? It wasn't like I could go too far, so maybe the changes wouldn't be that radical. Perhaps the universe one jump left didn't have oil. Maybe it wasn't an absence of things, maybe in the two jumps right universe homo sapiens and homo neanderthalensis had continued to coexist.

I turned away from the ATM and looked at my casket. It had been one of our more popular designs. I hadn't made plans for my funeral, so I guessed Michael must have chosen it.

'It's peaceful here,' I reflected. 'I'm sorry I didn't get to spend more time with you, here and back in the world.'

'Me too, but I liked being your brother.'

'I liked being your brother. If I could do that again I would. OK, I know what I am choosing.'

We smiled at each other, and I pulled Ernest into another smothering hug, pressing my face into his hair. When we broke apart, I kept hold of his hand, and clutching it, I turned and made my choice.

Some things that you need to be aware of when taking VRETx

Shabs Rajan

Since hooking up on VRETx, your life has taken a turn for the better.

WARNING: There are some side effects.

Your morning routine begins at 0500, face down on your recently varnished mahogany floor and after a hundred and seven push-ups and a few back and lateral stretches, paying special attention to your neck muscles, you leave for work. As you lock the door, you notice that the screaming from next door which kept you awake last night has ceased. You pause by your door, your head cocked ever so slightly, and reassure yourself that they have released Ashraf, his wife Sameera, and their kids, Saleem and Iman.

'They have released Ashraf, Sameera, Saleem and Iman,' you tell yourself.

'They have released Ashraf, Sameera, Saleem and Iman.'

As you drive out of your compound, you nod at the man with the Kalashnikov who flashes his yellow teeth at you with pride. But when you take a second look in the mirror (because you must check your surroundings not just once, not just twice but several times) he's gone.

You work at Harvey's Fitness Hell (because NO PAIN! NO GAIN!) where you were recently promoted to VP of Strength and Wellness. You don't know what it means but your 0700, a city type, whose hair remains wet and slick throughout his workout, values your new title and recommends you to his 'chums'. He used to be a marathon man until he ripped his cruciate and has since been trying to regain his strength. While you push him through the routines, the majority lower body workouts, leg presses, calf presses, thigh lifts, he talks big: new investments, long ones, short ones, derivatives,

42

which one will burst first, commodities or biotech?

He tells you how you should invest in something that only he has the expertise to manage and how he'd like to 'bang' his secretary but has resisted for fear of any sexual harassment stunt she could pull on him.

'There's no space left for men like us to be men anymore,' he grunts as he lifts 42.5 on the leg press. You watch the bone beneath the pale, pink skin, as his leg stiffens.

Burst. Which one will burst first?

A month into your second tour, before the shrapnel, before the psych evaluation, you saw a family in an overturned, simmering car by the side of the road. Scattered around them were their clothes, bags, potatoes. The mother was dead, and the boy sat at his father's side, obediently like he was at school. His father, who'd passed out, had his right leg trapped inside the cars metal carcass. When your platoon cut him out, the white bone of the femur jutted out through his brown skin like a chicken bone in thick, red, and creamy sauce. You gagged but held it in and then, when you were sure no one was watching, you threw up back at the barracks. But only that first time.

Sometimes, as your 0700 drools over his secretary while lifting his feather weights, you want to move that pin to a hundred kilos, just to see his leg snap, the gleaming white of the bone and the surprise in his eyes. No PAIN! No GAIN!

VRETx is instrumental in keeping that pin where it is, you tell yourself.

VRETx has helped you overcome your difficulties, you tell yourself.

VRETx is the reason you are who you are today.

A lifetime ago, after your father had a heart attack working at the docks, after you moved in with your step-dad and then broke his nose when he tried to take a swing at you, after you blinded some fat cunt in a bar fight, a fight that you instigated because you called him a wanker, they packed you off to where every idiotic, racist, second-rate shit-for-brains-citizen goes when no one else wants them. As you popped insurgents, one by one, you forgot about everything else. You found your purpose as you looked for survivors amongst buildings razed to the ground by high end drone missiles. You engaged with the locals at their fruit stalls and, later, after car bombs ripped through the market, you would try and not step on them, as they lay holding their guts. The squish of watermelon and papaya in blood, the smell of burning flesh.

Between clients you wait in the Chill Zone, sipping sparkling water, keeping your eyes fixed on the bubbles as they try to rush up the bottle's neck. Around you, people shuttle from reception to changing room to studio to showers, their trainers squeaking on the smooth, waxed floor, as they casually glide over craters, and mines, unaware of the underground tunnels where insurgents hide. Someone says hello; you look up and smile, and then turn your attention back to the bottle. Relationships are better limited to one. Preferably, none.

An announcer, in a nice, calm voice says that Cyclomaniacs with

44

Jean-Luc is about to begin and that everyone who signed up should make their way to Studio 5. Several clients run past you. A few without arms, one woman holding her head which is still in a hijab, an old man with flames leaping up his back. The water cooler may have exploded again. Loud thumping music vibrates and rattles your chair. The spinning has begun.

Your 1200 on a Wednesday is the highlight of your week. You notice that the bruise she conceals under her makeup is not as prominent as the one she carried last week. When she sees you studying her, she turns her head towards the red, digital clock on the wall.

'Come on,' she says. 'The clock is ticking.' She grins and then winces.

Once, when you were feeling weak and lonely, you followed her back to her semi-detached home with one garage, space for a second car up front, one dog and one swing in the back yard. You watched as she hugged her little girl who had sprinted out in a blue jumpsuit with yellow planets, as she waved goodbye to her Bangladeshi maid, as she cringed beside her husband and as they argued and, later, as they fought behind the curtains. There are marks where your fingers throttled the steering wheel.

When you were on your second tour, when shrapnel cut right through your six-pack, you had argued with your commander that you could still be out there. But you'd failed your psych test: Surpriiiiiise Soldier! You are still an idiotic, racist, second-rate shit-for-brains-citizen.

So, they shipped you back home, back to good old friends,

welcome back- parties, forget-the-past cocaine binges and thank-you-for-your-service sex. You were a hero until your fifteen minutes of fame ticked away, the coke slipped through your fingers, the sex dried up and those nightmares began. Nightmares that retained the smell of burning flesh, the crack of broken bones, a girl trying to shake her dead parents awake, a father running through the street carrying his child, begging you to do something as you stand there frozen, unable to move, just like in real life. You kept waking up in someone else's bed, next to someone whose name you couldn't remember, whose first question in the morning was 'Did we use a rubber?' or 'WHO THE FUCK ARE YOU?' or 'You still here?' or someone who just wanted to kick you out of bed onto the street, in a city hundreds of thousands of miles away where people could switch the channel when your hell appeared on Newsnight.

So where did that leave you? In a dive bar in Ealing Common, Bhangra blaring out of speakers, turbans walking round like they own the place, drinking you under the table. But you weren't there to make friends with those bastards. You were there because you heard that, now, after all these years, there's a way to get rid of pain. You heard about it on the dark-net and you finally found a guy who could hook you up to something known as VRETx.

Remy9 was all bones wrapped in yellow skin layered in ink, half assed shapes and pictures, after-thoughts on culture, race, language, and those were the ones not covered by his army greens. His eyes caved into his bald skull and those black circles around them were so prominent they looked like he'd crayoned them in.

Much later, when you have two episodes in a day, and you need more content and you break into his apartment wearing a balaclava,

46

beat him senseless, rob his stuff and leave him lying on the floor in his own piss and blood, you realise he is the way he is because he's so jacked up on VRETx, always in a permanent state of limbo, neither here in this awful reality nor in his own hell.

'So, you seen some bad shit and need some good stuff, eh?' he said, leaning close to you. Too close. His breath smelt of mints, which he popped every few minutes, standing up, reaching for them in his tight pants, offering them to you even though you'd declined the first time and blanked him every other. You didn't like him, but you didn't care because all you wanted to do was to try the goods. When you're buying another round of Jack's, he slips it in your coat (the beige one your dad wore to your graduation, the same day you made up some excuse about needing to be with your professors because you were too embarrassed to introduce him to your mates) and says, 'Place it where it hurts.'

You initially think this means up your arse and when you clarify, without looking at him, holding onto the bourbon he asked for, it's too late; he's long gone, behind the turbans and smoke.

Unable to wait any longer, you slipped into the john, ignored the shit and stink that greeted you and settled down on the rim to unwrap the cellophane and for an instant you thought, 'Oh my God I've been had.' Instead of finding a pouch of white powder or pills or brown rock, there was a pair of contact lenses, ear plugs, a mini-disc player and a metal slug the size of your thumb.

Place it where it hurts.

You lifted your shirt, searched for that scar on your waist, your very own shrapnel wound, placed the slug on it in disbelief, and waited.

It began to crawl around the scar and then you felt something slice into your skin. You tried to snatch it, but it was too late, and you bellowed as it burrowed its way into your wound, into your stomach, and someone banged on the door.

'You ok mate?'

'You ok?'

'You ok?'

'You ok?'

Of course you were.

You had never felt better.

As the contacts melted in your eyes and your gut tightened, the slug settled deep into you and the plugs crept into your ear canals. It felt like your very first crush except she was just feeding you endless supplies of butterflies, butterflies, butterflies. It was like that time you cranked up that Ferrari on the track which your friend had hired for his twenty fifth birthday and had invited you (but only because you were the only one without a full-time job). It was like the only time with Louisa Mar, who was older and more experienced than you, in the back seat of a red Ford Fiesta, parked at the Asda parking lot, only it was better because you were hard from the start and didn't come too soon. It was like your very first kill.

Now, from the comfort of your own one-bed flat, you can hear bones crack and snap, like popcorn in a microwave. You can walk past burning cars, shops, and splattered watermelon. You can turn up the sound just by thinking about it and children will screech louder, mothers will weep inconsolably while fathers hurl abuse - watch out - may turn out to be insurgents! You are where you belong. It's everything you hoped for and everything you need.

You have your first episode two weeks after the first time. Sitting on a bench at a park off King's Street. You watched kids scrambling up metal debris - or a plastic castle - and monkey bars that had been shattered by a rocket - not a rocket - which still lay in the ground. Parents, looking at their wrists, rubbing them as if time would go faster, cursed the sun which had gate crashed a winter's day.

There was no sun, but sweat had built up in your parka, trickled down your neck, into a pool at the small of your back. Did it slide down your ears and over the plugs? Did you feel those contacts melting in your eyes? Was there a slug creeping around in your guts? Can't be sure? On VRETx you can never be sure but that's why it's so good.

You were crouching behind the bench. For my husband James who enjoyed sitting here. From where you were you could see a girl with auburn hair on a swing. She wore a blue jumpsuit, patterned with yellow crescent moons, stars and planets. Her ponytails like strands of spaghetti swirled around her face, leaving only the white teeth and chin.

You were in the bushes. Watching. Waiting.

From somewhere, someone said, 'Target localised. Move'. It came from your right, and it sounded like sand being poured through your ears. You heard it before the pain hit.

But you tried to stay calm because you knew all of this was just in your head.

On your left, about a hundred metres away, a man with shaggy red hair, fiddled with his phone, his Kalashnikov, his phone, and looked up. To his immediate right, a brunette, light skinned, athletic, tall about 1.75, froze, her hands gripped the swing, the child was in midair, falling off. She looked like a puppet being thrown from a burning building, but she never hit the ground. The yellow sun, planets and crescent moon printed on the girl's blue jumpsuit flew off the cloth in the direction she swung, they floated in the air and remained there mid-flight. The colours deepened, the yellows became more yellow across the green background of the park, contrasted harshly against the blue sky.

There was a tightness in your gut, on the right above your waistline. Where the shrapnel cut your skin. Where the shrapnel still lies, proliferating. A swelling near your appendix. It was pulsing and felt like it would burst any second. Your head throbbed and someone stabbed you and you screamed.

When you were twelve, living with your stepdad, you needed an emergency appendectomy. Later when you were discharged, standing under the shower, fiddling with the bandage, the wound became infected, yellow pus oozed out and stank up your stepdad's plush apartment up in the Heath. He had to leave Match of the Day and your mother drunk on the carpet to rush you to hospital. 'You fucking stink you idiot!' he kept saying with his head out the car window like a shaggy, wet rottweiler. At the hospital, doctors came over to have a look. 'What's that smell, man? Jesus, man. What's that smell?' While you bit into a wooden spoon, someone cleaned your two-inch wound out with their fingers. Your legs had a mind of

50

their own; they kicked and kicked, like a horse being branded at the blacksmiths. With tears streaming down your face, your stepdad grabbed your shoulder and said, 'Man-up pussy. Man-up or you find your own place to live.'

You had never felt pain like that until the shrapnel.

And then you woke up on a smooth floor with brown, yellow, red bits of food, the taste of last night's curry sauce from Wang's in your mouth. The sound of running water and a gunfight in the background. You were lying naked on your bathroom floor with your head underneath the toilet. You don't know which day it was that you had that episode, but it doesn't matter because today you're VP of Strength and Wellness at Harvey's Fitness Hell.

Since you got hooked on VRETx your life has taken a turn for the better.

Thanks to VRETx you have no nightmares, you breathe easier and achieve deep sleep within minutes of plugging in. You work a 9 to 5 job at Harvey's Fitness Hell (because No Pain! No Gain!). Your mind is your temple, and it sits focused and ready atop its pedestal, your body. Your morning routine begins at 0500, face down on your recently varnished mahogany floor, with back and lateral stretches, paying special attention to your neck muscles.

Your 0700 is a city type who, one day, will need a wheelchair. But not today. Your 1200 is the highlight of your week. One day she'll find her husband in hospital unable to raise his arms. But not today. When she's ready, after she's done with him for good, she'll find the courage to invite you for a drink in the Chill Zone, where she might order a skinny café-latte that's served with tiny, caramel biscuits on the side for herself, while you settle for a sparkling water.

But you will politely decline the invitation because you need to limit your relationships to one.

On the way back from work, the motorway has come to a halt, streams of cars switch lanes to keep moving but then they all begin to crawl. There's an accident up ahead, fire truck, ambulances, police, the works – it doesn't look good. You catch a glimpse of a child whose screams you hear long before you drive past. Her mouth wide open, eyes shut, red splotches on her face, hands grasping the space between her and the driver, who you imagine is her mother, now probably catching her final breath behind the wheel. You actively seek her out in the gap between the police officer who is waving you past, the two firemen, one cutting the door, the other craning over his shoulder, and a medic soaking up the blood which had run up his arms.

In the oncoming lane, a lady in the car, at the top of the queue waiting to be let through, has turned around in her seat and is struggling to cover the eyes of her boy who's craning his head, curious, fixated on the scene. He must have a fire truck just like that at home. You fix your stare on that boy as you drive past, willing him to keep his eyes open.

And just as you move past, the sun streams in, the landscape turns to sand and a man in rags - watch out! - points his Kalashnikov at you and flashes his yellow teeth with pride.

Since hooking up on VRETx, your life has taken a turn for the better.

WARNING: There are some side effects.

Broken Crayons

Janet Armstrong

South London 1981

'Miss, there's a kid tyin' 'imself to the railings!'

The whole of 3b crowds round the first-floor window and peers down at the black railings in front of the school. Miss Taub heaves her shoulders and gives off a sigh. She doesn't bother barking at them to sit back down. They're not laughing or pointing; they just can't believe what they're seeing.

The kid in question has removed his blazer, pullover and shirt and has used them to fashion a makeshift rope he's tied around his naked midriff and lashed to the railings. Over a huddle of teenage heads, Miss Taub watches Mr Eastwick waving his arms around in the air, and through the classroom din she can just about make out a few serious words being flung around outside. She shakes her head; from the way the boy was behaving earlier in the day, she knows any efforts at dissuading him will be futile.

*

Keith wasn't into the idea of school that day. It was too early in the morning, his head ached, and his hands stung with cold. He pulled frayed sleeves over his fingers to cover his chapped knuckles and stuffed his hands deep into his blazer pockets, pulling his arms close to his body.

Everett threw him a sideways glance and nudged him with the end of a sharp pencil. 'You're s'posed to be writin' the words in your book, you dipshit.'

Keith turned his face away. He didn't want to write any words. He wanted to tell Everett to shove his words up his stuck-up little arse, but as soon as he began to speak, his stomach gurgled, and his face began to burn. If Everett saw his face flush, he'd point and the whole class would turn and stare, so he buried his head in his chest and said nothing.

The teacher was stood at the board pointing at badly drawn pictures of food. She wanted the class to repeat German words for sausage and ice cream, but Keith couldn't focus; the words were a chalky blur and made him hungry. He sucked in his stomach muscles, huffed and stared at Miss Taub. She had a long face like a horse and greasy ginger hair pulled up in a lank ponytail. Keith wasn't sure if German people were supposed to look like that. The ones in the pictures from World War Two were different; they had shiny golden hair and triangular faces like the posh sandwiches you got at birthday parties.

Keith thought about those sandwiches: grated Cheddar cheese and chunks of spicy pickle, slices of ham smeared with hot mustard, crunchy slivers of cucumber with pink salmon paste. His mouth started to water. He breathed in as hard as he could and looked up at the clock behind the board: 9.15. He watched the second-hand jerk awkwardly around the circular face of the clock and squeezed his stomach muscles a little tighter. Another forty-five minutes of German and then Maths before break. Maths – that was the woman with the acne face that made him want to puke and the scratchy voice that reminded him of the feel of wool on his bare skin.

Everett prodded Keith in the ribs with his finger and stabbed at Keith's rough book with his freshly sharpened pencil. 'Words, you thick piece of smelly shit!'

Keith shuffled his buttocks around on the wooden chair to expel some wind, rubbed his flank where the finger had gone in and checked the clock again. The long hand was dangling somewhere between the 3 and the 4.

On most days, Keith liked Miss Taub; she had a generous smile and would stop to speak to him in the corridor at break. She'd even given him a piece of chocolate cake once when he'd had no lunch. He'd thought it tasted like brown velvet – if velvet could have a taste. It made the inside of his stomach feel warm and tingly. But today he just wasn't feeling it, and he just couldn't budge that gooey, warm chocolate cake puffy cloud of a dream out of his mind.

'Keith,' she said. 'How would you ask for a glass of milk in a German café?'

All he heard was milk - all warm, brown with cocoa, and bubbly with marshmallows on top. Milk with hundreds and thousands swimming around in it leaving a rainbow-coloured trail behind them that he could stir with his finger and lick clean. That was exactly how Keith's gran had served it up.

Keith pushed the thought from his mind. He groaned and shook his head. 'I dunno, Miss.'

'Keith, try,' she urged, pushing an oily strand of red hair out of her eye. 'Du mußt versuchen.'

'I can't.'

Everett tittered. 'You dumb fuck,' he sniggered, and prodded Keith in the side with his pencil, digging it in with a twist. 'My mum says you're poor. Is that why you stink?' He clamped his fingers around his nose like a peg and tittered again.

'Keith,' the teacher said. 'Repeat...ich möchte ein Glas Milch, bitte.'

Keith turned to her and began, 'Ish mosh...' He tried hard to copy the words, but the image of the chocolate cake inside his mind was too vivid, too powerful and too strong. He could smell the powdery icing sugar and taste the lush, thick cocoa on the tip of his tongue. 'Miss, 'ave you got any more of that chocolate cake you 'ad the other day?'

'Chocolate cake?' said Everett, sitting up in his chair. 'She gave you fuckin' chocolate cake?'

'Everett, that's enough,' replied an unflinching Miss Taub, her voice like ice.

The pencil twisted further into Keith's side, accompanied by a hefty kick in the shin that made his eyes water. He tugged at his sleeves and clenched his teeth, but the pencil drove deeper still. He felt something warm and sticky run down his side, but he didn't want to look under his jumper in case Everett saw and kicked him again.

'Keith,' said Miss Taub briskly, placing a wedge of roughly sliced Banda sheets in front of the boy. 'Hand out these worksheets, will you? Oh, and get the crayon tray out of the cupboard. Everett, can you hand out the scissors?'

Everett rose from his seat and headed to the cupboard, 'I'll be back,' he whispered in Keith's ear. 'Don't go thinkin' I'm finished wiv you.'

Keith took the wedge of purple printed sheets, held them to his nose, inhaled, and began tossing them onto the tables. The sweetly pungent odour reminded him of violets and the coloured candy flowers his gran'd used to put on top of little spongey fairy cakes. He'd stolen a whole tub of them from her cupboard once and eaten every single one. She hadn't even noticed, and now he felt guilty every time he thought of it.

If Gran had still been there, they could put bets on the horses on Saturday morning and watch the races on the telly in the afternoon with a plate of bramble jelly sandwiches and a thick chunk of madeira cake. He might even win a little pocket money and she'd let him keep it. He'd even picked the winner at Aintree last year – Ben Nevis it was called. 'You won, Keith. You're a clever lad,' she'd said, bouncing up and down on her armchair. 'You're my little winner. I should call you Ben, not Keith, shouldn't I?' She'd chuckled at her own joke, rolling her eyes in that funny way that'd always made him laugh.

Everett handed out the scissors – plonking a pair on every desk with a sharp snapping sound – and returned to his seat. Keith finished distributing the Banda sheets, took the crayon tray from the cupboard and sat down with it still in front of him.

'You're s'posed to hand out the crayons, you fuckin' crank, not sit an' stare at 'em,' said Everett with a lopsided grin on his face, and he lifted his scissors, pointing them at Keith in a circular motion, jabbing at him like a clumsy boxer.

'Keith, hand out the crayons, please,' said Miss Taub from the front of the room. She was scratching something on the board with chalky fingers. Keith couldn't work out how she did that – how could she see what he was doing without turning round, and how come she never saw what that git Everett was doing?

Everett leant over and drove the scissors through Keith's jumper and into his side, giving them a twist. 'That's for the cake, yer nasty little swot.' He twisted again, but the other way. 'That one's for yer dead granny,' and he laughed like a demon.

Pain shot up Keith's side, cannoned into his neck and smacked straight into his frontal lobes, where something snapped - just like a cheap toothpick - the kind you got in Chinese restaurants. He took a thick, red crayon from the tray, lifted the V of Everett's jumper and stuffed it down his neck, pressing it as hard as he could into his chest. 'You're a nasty little shit,' he hissed. 'Don't talk about my gran like that.'

Miss Taub lurched forward and reached for the crayon tray, but she wasn't quick enough. Keith stood up and rained the room with a barrage of crayons. A waxy rainbow hurtled into each corner of the room and onto every desk, the colours merging in wide arched ribbons of every hue. He watched as Everett screamed and ducked under the table; hands clasped together over a cluster of blond curls.

'Keith,' said Miss Taub coldly. 'Keith, calm down, please.' She bent to pick up a handful of crayons from the floor, but the tray was still half full, and Keith didn't want to call a truce when things were going his way.

'Miss, stop 'im,' pleaded the row of girls at the back of the class. 'It's scarin' us.'

'Keith,' began Miss Taub again, but her pleas fell upon deaf ears. A dark shadow had draped itself over the boy's face like a shroud. He felt different, stronger, more powerful, like Ben Nevis. Like his gran'd old him he'd be.

He reached for the scissor tray.

'Keith, that's not...' said Miss Taub, shaking her head.

'No way,' he said. A frisson of pride rippled through his body as he detected a frown scud momentarily over the woman's face. He flexed a skinny arm like a catapult, and a hail of green-handled scissors ricocheted like machine gun fire around the classroom. It felt mechanical - almost robotic - and his stomach didn't gurgle anymore. Was this how it felt to be Everett? Was this how Ben Nevis'd felt when he crossed the finishing line at Aintree?

'Right, everybody out. Alphabetical order,' said Miss Taub, opening the classroom door. 'Elizabeth - go to the head's office and tell him to come immediately.' Then, turning to Keith, 'Stay here and wait for Mr Eastwick.'

Keith watched as 1c lined up and filed their way out into the corridor. Miss Taub was calling out orders. 'Everett Yates, get to the back of the line. Isabel Adams, you're first, then Matthew. We'll continue in the library until the head comes.'

Then they disappeared and Keith was alone.

'You can do it, Keith,' said a voice inside his head. 'You're a winner, remember? You could be on top of the world, like Ben Nevis.'

'Yes, Gran,' he said. She was right, as she'd always been. He was a winner. He could fight that little prick Everett Yates anytime he wanted. He'd seen the way Everett'd screamed like a girl.

'Go on, Keith,' said Gran's voice again. 'I bet there's cake in Miss Taub's cupboard. Eat it. Go on. It'll be like tea on Saturdays.'

Chocolate cake – all sticky and fudgy, satisfying and warm. Keith dropped the scissors and slid open the drawers to Miss Taub's desk. In the bottom one, he found what he was looking for – a large, plastic tub labelled Teatime Assortment.

'You deserve it, Keith. Eat it.'

He peeled back the lid, threw it frisbee-style onto the carpet and dug his fingers into the soft lush, spongey bounty, cramming chunks of it into his mouth, throwing his head back and letting the crumbs tumble off his lips and down the faded lapels of his blazer. He gouged at it again and took a second mouthful, and a third and a fourth, until his face was scored with rich brown streaks and only a few stray crumbs remained in the tub.

'Why should you be left behind, Keith?' said Gran's voice. 'You've done nothing wrong.'

Keith wasted no time. He scooped up the last few crumbs from the tub, stuffed them in his pockets and headed for the library. He wasn't going to wait for that dick of a headmaster. He was a winner. He was on top of the mountain, on top of the whole fucking world.

'What a lovely class you have there, Miss,' remarked the librarian, smiling as 1c filed in.

Miss Taub smiled back as she ticked off each name from her register, taking care to pencil only a question mark next to Keith's name.

Keith hid behind the library doors. He stood on tiptoes and peered at Miss Taub through the glass panels in the library doors.

'You can all practice being in a German café until Mr Eastwick says we can go back to the classroom,' she was saying, motioning at the tables. 'Sit down in groups of four. One of you can be the waiter, and the others can be customers. Jetzt los!'

'One Milkshake, bitte,' he heard Everett say. The sound of his voice grated on him like the sound of Miss Taub's stubby nails on the blackboard.

'Moshten Sie nock etwas?' replied Matthew.

'Ya, one shtook Schokoladencake for...' began Everett.

A cloud formed on Keith's face and brewed up a storm.

THUD.

The heavy doors hit the walls and the sound echoed out like thunder into the mouth of the long corridor and beyond. Keith crashed through the doors and cartwheeled clumsily through the bookshelves and onto Everett's table, kicking a few carefully positioned books out of place along the way.

'Show the teacher what the little git did,' said Gran's voice.

Keith stood proud atop the table and lifted his jumper to show a bloodied shirt underneath. 'That was 'im, an' 'is pencil,' he said, looking at Miss Taub. He dug his finger in the wound and pointed at Everett with a bloodied nail. 'Little Lord Fauntleroy. He done it.'

CLACK.

A medium-sized man with steel-rimmed spectacles and notable underarm sweat patches appeared in the doorway. He looked up at Keith.

'Get down from the table,' he said in a low tone. 'Or I'm calling your father. You've got five seconds. One, two...'

Keith peeled off his blazer and jumper and unbuttoned his shirt. He swung them around his head like a stripper and waggled his hips for effect like he'd seen on Morecambe and Wise.

'Three, four...'

'FIVE,' said Keith, standing bare-chested on the table. The winter sun sliced its way through the big windows, making the flat white surface of his meagre chest shine like a pearl.

Mr Eastwick stared. The moisture patches under his arms were expanding and a light mist gathered on the edges of his spectacles.

'I'm not comin' down.' Keith began to unbuckle the belt of his trousers, then stared back at the headteacher. 'You can beg all you like, but I'm not.'

Mr Eastwick smoothed back his hair with a sweaty hand and said, 'Keith, if you stop this now, we can forget all about it, but...' He paused to look at Keith's classmates sat around the tables. Not one of them moved a muscle, their eyes fixed on the thin sparrow of a figure standing, legs akimbo, on the table.

'Nah,' said Keith. He looked Mr Eastwick square in the eyes, unbuckled his belt and started to slip it through the loops on his pants.

'Show them who's boss,' said Gran.

'Keith, that's not a good idea,' said Mr Eastwick, taking a step forward and raising one hand.

'No,' said Keith again, and he waved the liberated belt around in the air like a snake.

'Sssssss,' he hissed, holding the buckle like a snake's head.

Mr Eastwick rubbed his temples and said, 'Come down, Keith, or we'll have to ring your father.'

'Father?' snorted Keith, making wild S shapes in the air with the belt. 'Since when did 'e care? 'E'll be in the Red Lion anyway, or down the bookies.'

He hissed again, drawing his lips back from his teeth like an angry bull terrier.

Miss Taub took a deep breath and said, 'You'll get expelled, Keith. No more chocolate cake.'

'Good,' said Keith. 'This school's shit, anyway.' He looked at Mr Eastwick. 'You're shit, Sir.' A trace of a smile appeared on his lips.

Mr Eastwick sighed and glanced at the clock on the wall. 'Keith, this has been going on too long. I think it's time for you to pack it in, don't you? I'll call your dad and he can take you home.'

'Nah,' said Keith. 'I'm not going 'ome. He's shit, and you're shit.' He turned to look at Miss Taub. 'She's shit as well. Even with 'er cakes.'

He looked around the room at his classmates and said, 'You're all shit an' all.'

Not one of them moved.

Mr Eastwick glanced quickly at Miss Taub and said, 'Keith, this is your last chance. If you don't stop, I'll have to...'

He didn't finish. Keith had already kicked off his shoes, flung his belt on the table and unzipped his pants.

'Not a chance,' said Keith. His trousers fell to his ankles in a puddle of tatty black cloth, and he stood there, on the library table, dressed only in a pair of off-white underpants and a pair of holey grey socks.

'Keith,' said Miss Taub.

'Get lost,' he said, and gathering the pile of clothes in a pair of skinny white arms, he jumped down from the table, his socked feet making a light thud on the floor.

'Hisssss,' he said again, waving the belt at his classmates, and walked proudly out of the double doors into the corridor, still waggling his hips.

'Well done, my little winner,' said Gran. 'You won, like Ben Nevis.'

*

Miss Taub glances up at the clock on the wall: 2.15pm. He's been there nearly all day, and the temperature outside can't be far above zero.

'He's got no trousers on, Miss. That's indecent, that is.'

She breathes in, shrugs her shoulders and joins 3b at the

66

window. Mr Eastwick's sweat patches have reached his waist and his shirt clings to his back like a damp dishcloth. The boy's father is clutching the railings and saying something. He has a craggy, unshaven face with unkempt greying hair, and a cigarette hangs from his bottom lip. He takes his coat off and tries to drape it around the boys' shoulders, but the boy bats it away and it slumps to the floor. He slaps the boy around the face. Miss Taub doesn't hear the sound it makes, but she knows it hurts as the boy turns his cheek away and spits on the floor.

Mr Eastwick is saying something. Miss Taub can't make out the words, but the boy's face is unmoving. It still bears the streaks of the chocolate cake he stole from her desk. She doesn't begrudge him that; she can make another cake, but she wishes he would give up and go home.

''e must be freezin', Miss'.

'What's 'e protestin' about, Miss?'

'Why's 'e doin' that?'

She smiles, shakes her head and says she doesn't know anything. She glances up at the clock again: 2.45. He'll have to give up soon. Fifteen minutes until the last bell of the day and she has a date with Mr Carlsson later.

A white car draws up outside.

'It's the cops, Miss.'

She cups her chin in her hand and peers out of the window. She guesses Mr Eastwick's patience has run out.

3b huddle closer around the window. Two police officers cut

through the makeshift rope lashed to the railings and carry the boy away between them, his pipe cleaner legs waggling around in the air like a duck out of water. She sees his face through the rear window of the police car. He looks up at her and then looks away again as the car pulls away. She knows that's the last time she'll see Keith. He's not the first and he won't be the last. She picks up the plastic tub from the floor, replaces the lid and places it on her desk.

She looks up at the clock. It's 14.59. The bell rings, she dismisses 3b and looks around.

The floor is littered with broken crayons.

Wooden Horses

Juliet Robinson

The city walls stretch high into the sky; in the skirmish around the gate, they are the horizon. The scrum of bodies presses forward, and I go with it, unable to do anything else. I've lost my shield, but so many of my fellows have theirs raised that it makes little difference, I am still sheltered from the crap that is being flung from the walls. In fact, having no shield seems to be beneficial; I can pay more attention to my footing. It's so easy to stumble and fall, to be trampled under the weight of armoured men. Many soldiers have died here, crushed beneath the feet of their comrades.

Next to me, Obasi swears constantly as he braces under the impact of falling items.

'Fuck Agamemnon, fuck Menelaus, fuck Achilles, fuck Odysseus, fuck Nestor,' and on and on. At the start of the war, he had cursed those behind the wall, but Obasi has lost two sons to this conflict; he is a changed man, and his battle mantra reflects this.

A shattering crash sounds up ahead; something huge has been tossed down onto the shields. The formation splits apart under its weight and by the Gods, whatever it is, it stinks. In front of us the shield wall comes undone, as men turn tail and run. Blood and sweat froth the air, and the stench of rot permeates all. I gag and in that second, I lose my footing, stumbling over an abandoned shield. Suddenly the crowd which had moments ago been an organised fighting unit is stampeding and I am tossed under their feet.

Once you are downed on the field it is near impossible to get up. I try but fail. It seems that every man fleeing the gates manages to trample over me. I quickly give up trying to regain my feet and instead slither forward. Something that is fairly easy as the ground is churned up and blood-soaked.

And then something smashes into my head, my helm is knocked clean off and the world rings like a thunderclap. Stunned I lie panting on the ground, no longer even able to shield myself from the retreating feet of my fellows. I take the blows, the broken ribs, the crushed wrist, the hair ripped from my scalp. If I am left here, I will die. Having not wanted to waste their arrows earlier, the archers would soon be up on the wall picking off the injured and the dying.

I must do something. I hoarsely call for help but my cries go unanswered.

The vile stench from earlier swamps the air, causing my vision to blur. I roll onto my side and vomit. My surroundings have fallen still; I have been left behind at the gates with just the dead and the dying for company.

A few feet from me lies the rotted carcass of a horse. This ruined beast is what smashed our shield formation. I pull myself to it, my body protesting bitterly as I do so. It is split open, blasted apart and like a maggot I wriggle inside the rotting beast, scooping out its innards as I go, hollowing out a space for myself. The smell now encompasses everything. I retch and choke, but I am determined to live. Burrowed inside the knackered beast I lay still, curled between its ribs.

The sun is high, and it bears down mercilessly. I bake in the horse's body while around me the calls, cries, and moans of those left behind on the field are silenced by arrows from the wall. I am a child again, alone in the night, wishing for my mother, who has been sold.

I stew among rotting guts. As the day wears on, I consider leaving my sanctuary; death would be swift and merciful compared to this misery. But I don't. Slowly the temperature begins to drop, though the stench of the horse never lessens.

First dusk, then night covers the churned-up field in front of the Scaean Gates. Stiffly I scramble from my rotten den, a fog of flies scattering around me. I stagger to my feet, ridged with the expectation that arrows will thud into my back. But none do. Thanking the Gods, I stumble away, back towards the beach and safety.

Guards shout challenges as I approach the camp's ditch.

'Greek! Greek!' I call in a parched voice.

Spears are thrust at my chest and neck. Faces, pale in the lantern light loom and then someone splutters and chokes.

'By the Gods, what have you been rolling in Pelias?' Obasi guffaws. 'You smell worse than the camp dogs!' The spears are lowered, and I push past the guards into the camp. Obasi falls into step beside me. 'We counted you dead, but yet you walk and appear to live.'

'I spent my day in the body of a rotted horse.' I shudder and continue straight towards the sea. Through the camp I go, round the fires, tents, middens and then into the rolling waves. I don't stop till they lap my shoulders, then I allow myself to sink beneath the water, letting the salted ocean clean some of my stench away. The current pushes me back towards the beach and I let it. The cool water sooths my aches, and I lie on the sand with the waves slowly washing over me.

Obasi watches me, leaning on his spear. He has a fresh, jagged cut running across his face but is otherwise fine. Eventually I pick myself up.

'I'm going to the bathing tents and when I am done, I am going to eat until my stomach feels fit to burst,' I inform my friend. He follows along, pestering me with questions, but I brush them off. I haven't the energy. What I want is a soak, to oil myself and forget about the discomfort of the past day.

I take my time in the bathing tent and on several occasions, I bat away the comforting hands of slave girls. Ordinarily I would have been grateful for their salve, but not tonight. I return to barracks and dress in a fresh tunic. My old one is abandoned, and my armour will take days to clean. I will probably discard it and face the wrath of the quartermasters. It seems unlikely the stench of the cooked and rotten horse will ever be truly cleaned from it. I swear I can smell it now, lingering on my skin and hair, though I scrubbed myself raw.

No matter the hour, there is always food to be had in the camp. Vendors have set up stalls, there is a market and of course the soldiers' kitchens. I make my way to the main mess but stop on the way to buy some shellfish from a vendor, who boils them in a broth ladened with garlic. I crave their strong taste; I hope it will chase away the one of bile that lingers in my throat. When I arrive at the mess, it's near empty. A few drunk spearmen are there but other than that, the long wooden tables are vacant. I load a plate with mutton stew, breads, olives and watered-down wine then set about sating myself.

When I am halfway through my meal, a group of men arrive.

They pester the cooks, demanding loukoumades which aren't yet ready. They are loud, buoyant and full of themselves. I crouch over my food and hope they will take benches far from me. But luck is not on my side.

'Pelias!' someone shouts.

I cringe. I am tired and I can't be bothered with drunks. A bottom slams onto the bench beside me and the brown face of Yiannis grins at me. His eyes reel and he struggles to sit upright.

'I heard that you did something strange with a horse!'

'Yeah, ha, ha,' I grumble. Of course, Obasi has been busy telling everyone about my adventure. I mean I would laugh if it hadn't been me in the reeking beast. I cram more food in my mouth, eager to be finished and away to my bed.

Yiannis's friends join us at the table, and I am surprised to see Janus, son of Patroclus is among their number. Patroclus is one of Achilles five commanders, his greatest friend and lover. Janus is a respected warrior in his own right but is known to have a love of dice games; he lost his chariot team recently to a bad roll.

'This is Pelias, who was birthed by a horse today!' Yiannis nudges Janus, as he roars with laughter, but Janus doesn't join in his mirth. He regards me with discerning brown eyes and a frown upon his brow.

'Do I wish to know the details?' he asks dubiously.

I speak before Yiannis can further embellish his tale.

'I got left behind at the gates today and I hid in the remains of a horse,' I sigh wearily. 'When the sun set, I made it back to camp.' I pick an olive from my plate and shoot a dirty look at Yiannis.

'Well, that's one way to survive,' Janus says thoughtfully. 'Disguise yourself as a dead horse.'

I am grateful that he doesn't seem to find my unpleasant day as funny as everyone else does.

'Yeah, shame we can't use such trickery to help us win the war,' Yiannis giggles. Then with a note of drunken cunning in his voice he continues, 'We could dress up as goats and goat herds and request entrance to the city. They must be desperate to replenish their herds.'

I finish my food and glower at the men sitting around me laughing. As I stand to leave, I notice Janus isn't laughing, he sits with a thoughtful look upon his face. The next few days, I am the brunt of every joke, but slowly it starts to blow over. We don't attack the gates or the city walls. It is hot, there is no breeze and none of our generals seem to have the energy for it. We train on the beach. We eat, we drink, and a caravan of traders pass through the camp. Life continues.

I am minding my own business one day, having just finished akratisma, when a group of armed Myrmidons approach me. I stare at them, uncertain. Patroclus is in their number and when someone points to me, I wish the ground would swallow me, though of course it doesn't oblige.

As they near, I stand to attention and bow my head. Patroclus is not my commander, but he is revered and loved by many. I grudgingly respect the man.

'Pelias come with us,' he says. He turns and leaves, not bothering to see if I will follow, which of course I do. His men flank me and lead me through the camp to the section where Achilles has garrisoned his people. Like the rest of the encampment, it is well-established, wooden structures have long since replaced tents. Several sparring rings form the focus of the social spaces and even the slaves have a well-built barracks. I notice that there are fewer stray dogs here and the people seem cleaner and better fed.

We come to an area of workshops, where armourers and carpenter's toil. The warm air smells of sawdust and sweat, saws bite into wood and hammers bang and thud. A huge trolley is being built with wheels taller than a man. I stare at it and wonder why I have been brought here.

Patroclus watches the craftsmen as they work. This is the first time I have been close to him. Normally, he is a distant figure on the battlefield. He is shorter without his helm, stockier than expected and his bare skin is covered with scars.

'You inspired this Pelias,' he says.

I frown, 'Excuse my ignorance, but I don't follow.'

'A ruse. We are building a wooden horse with which we shall take Troy.' I stare at him blankly and he roars with laughter. 'The horse is going to be large enough to hide myself and a few men inside. Not unlike you in your dead steed,' he smiles. 'We'll need to figure out how to convince the Trojans to accept this fine gift and wheel it inside their walls. Then under the cover of night, we can take the gates and throw the city open to the army.'

I flush with pride. My desperate act may have inspired something

76

that could end this bloody war.

'I want to help build it. I want to be in it!' I say, surprising myself.

'Of course you do, and I promise you shall be one of the chosen men,' Patroclus replies clapping a hand on my shoulder.

Later that day, I move to Achilles's camp. Obasi comes with me, as he had once been a carpenter's apprentice. Slowly the horse starts to rise from the sawdust. It will be huge once it is complete, and I wonder how the Trojans will get it through their gates.

Life in Achilles's camp is different. Patroclus and the other generals run the place well. The slaves are properly fed and cared for, and the stray dogs whose absence I had noted are here, but they have been made pets and are used to control the rat population.

Achilles hasn't left his house since his spat with Agamemnon about Briseis, the war prize and concubine. He sulks in the dark and to me it seems that his ill temper threatens to overwhelm the camp. Patroclus tries to counter it with overpowering good humour. Menesthius and the other generals are always trying to tempt their leader out with games and celebrations, but it never works. Everyone seems on edge; they tiptoe around Achilles. He only allows Patroclus into his house and has forbidden the female slaves from attending to him. But the most noticeable thing is that none of the soldiers he commands join in the skirmishes anymore. I wonder about Patroclus's plan and why he is pushing ahead with it. I doubt Achilles gave it his blessing. Perhaps he hopes it will jolt his friend out of his depression.

A few weeks after I move to Achilles's camp, a wild storm rolls in off the sea. The waves are high, and they wash far up the beach, smashing into the sections of the camp closest to the shore. We are high and dry but all around us is chaos. Men are drowning, horses are screaming, and fires have broken out. Lightning flashes, and it seems Zeus himself has come to intervene in our war. Achilles stumbles from his dark lair and roars at the sky. He delights and revels in the chaos. I watch him as everyone else scrambles to help those who have been struck by the waves. He is urging Zeus on. He shouts prayers to the god, beseeching him to help the Trojans, to lay waste to Agamemnon and return his honour.

Patroclus tries to calm Achilles, but he strikes him across the face, sending him reeling back. They stand and stare at each other, one hurt and the other burning with rage.

Thunder booms and a cry goes out that the gates are open, and the warriors of Troy are coming.

'Tomorrow, we sail for Greece!' Achilles barks an animal-like laugh and returns to his pit.

Around me men are running and all I do is turn on the spot, unsure of how to be of use. Suddenly Patroclus is there; he grabs my arm and demands my aid. He tows me along, shouting orders to others as we go and then we are at the armoury. He drags me inside and makes straight for the table where Achilles's armour is laid out. He begins to dress, shouting at me to help him, which I do with clumsy fingers.

Once the armour is on, Patroclus stands in the gloom, his face pensive and shadowed. I pass him Achilles's plumed helm and he disappears beneath its visor, becoming his friend and lover. He turns, a swirl of red cloak and marches into the storm. I follow on his heels like a loving dog. Outside he is greeted by roars of excitement. The men believe their leader has returned. Thunder and lightning battle in the sky while on the beach Greeks and Trojans fight for their lives.

The Myrmidons rush to arm themselves. They have missed the fight and are keen to blood their blades.

'Stay here, make sure Achilles doesn't find out about this,' Patroclus, now Achilles beseeches me.

'I promise,' I reply, wondering exactly how he expects me to do that.

The night is long, and the fighting is fierce. Runners bring news constantly and although I greet them at the gates of Achilles's encampment, I don't let them pass on inside. Once they have gone, I run to the door of Achilles's house and shout my censored version of the events through the door. Of course, I do not mention that Achilles is there at the thick of the battle, the spear head of the warriors.

A runner comes, a boy maybe six years old, his face a mask of shock and terror, 'Achilles! Achilles is dead!' he cries. 'Euphorbus wounded him then Hector himself slayed him, stabbing him through the stomach with his spear. The Myrmidons are fighting for his body.'

I turn to cold ash. I have aided in this deceitful play; I have had a hand in the death of Patroclus. On halting feet I go to relay the news to Achilles, my tongue swollen, my mouth dry, and my mind absent of any explanation.

'Sir,' I quaver and stall. My mind is racing. Should I weave excuses, lies, or tell the truth. And if I tell the truth how much of it should I share? Did anyone other than Patroclus know my part in this. 'Sir, they are reporting your death on the field.'

The door flies open and Achilles stares down at me. I cringe away from him; his eyes are merciless.

'Explain!' he roars. Then he notices the empty encampment. 'Where are my men?'

'Patroclus ordered me to remain here, to attend you. Your men, they went to fight the Trojans. I know nothing more. A runner came, he said you had fallen. I checked the armoury, and your armour is gone.' I nearly continue, almost go further with my lie. But experience has taught me it is better to keep untruths simple.

He pushes past me and bounds over to the armoury.

'Who? Who is wearing my armour?' he demands.

'I don't know. Things were confused, people were running everywhere, and the storm was at its fiercest. Patroclus ordered me to remain here.' I reiterate my order, afraid that Achilles will brand me a coward as well as a murderer.

'Patroclus,' he speaks the name softly as understanding flashes across his face. Then he is clutching his spear and rushing away through the camp, roaring and cursing the gods as he goes. He has finally re-joined the war.

As dawn settles the Greek army returns, Achilles amongst them, his face a mask of grief and pain. He carries in his arms the body of Patroclus. My heart rips and breaks. I had not long known Patroclus, but he was a good man, one of the best. Though this is not why I grieve. I grieve because of Achilles's pain. We all do.

Achilles bathes and cleans Patroclus's body himself, then lays him out in the small courtyard at the centre of his home. For days he rests there and Achilles refuses to listen to reason, to allow anyone to take his body and perform the proper burial rights.

We ghost around the encampment. We speak in whispers, even the dogs no longer bark. We fret that Patroclus may return demanding peace and to be allowed to pass on to Hades.

On the fourth day I wake to the smell of burning. Obasi and I rush to rise. A fire in this timber and cloth camp would be disastrous. I struggle into my tunic and join the others rushing to the source of the flames, the workshops.

There stands Achilles. He has set the horse Patroclus had been building alight. Through the heat haze I can discern a body laid between the legs of the horse. The grief worn warrior takes his knife and cuts his hair. He throws the shorn locks into the fire. One by one we stepped forward, taking the knife from Achilles and we shed our hair into the flames. Each cut lock symbolising the sundering of the dead from the living.

The horse burns for hours. In the morning when the fire is cold, I see Achilles gathering the ashes from the centre of the pyre where Patroclus was consumed by the flames. He pours these remains into a golden urn then turns to me.

'When I die, my ashes are to be joined with his.'

The war intensifies, driven purely by Achilles's grief. Hundreds die on both sides, Obasi is one of them. I wish this war over as I watch my friend's funeral pyre burn. Janus is there and I remember his father and the horse.

As the flames die, I approach him. He looks older and his brown eyes are troubled. We are all spent by this war.

'Let us finish this. Let's build your father's horse and take the city.'

We work on the horse like men possessed. Achilles is with us. He is determined to honour Patroclus, to revenge him with the death of Hector. There is no plan for how we shall get the horse behind the walls, but still, we build her. Achilles names her Nycteus, after Patroclus's mare and one of the four horses that draws Hade's chariot. She will bring death to Troy. So, the name is appropriate on two counts.

Word reaches Agamemnon about our endeavour, and he visits our camp. I hide in the shade of a workshop and watch the king as he inspects our work. He is impressed. He claps Achilles on the shoulder, then they embrace. Seemingly all is forgiven.

That night we feast with the King. I sit on a bench surrounded by heroes. Men who I have never respected, men who I blame for the death of my fellows, my friends. I am a hypocrite. I drink their wine, eat their food and despite the hope that this war may soon be over, I still hate them. I look over at Achilles. I don't despise him. You can't watch a man's heart break and not harbour a gentler emotion for him. His hands are as worn as mine from the carpentry of the horse. We have both bled and lost people we love here on the sands of Troy. He is a flawed man, but I now follow him with all my heart.

As the feast draws on Nestor, often considered to be wise by his fellows, stands.

'I have a solution for our horse and wall problem. We must depart, send our ships away.' Voices murmur dissent, but he continues, raising his own so it rises above them all. 'The Trojans will believe we have gone, but they will be wrong. We shall dig trenches and hide our men out on the plain. We shall hide them in the ditches, we shall hide them in the ruins of our camp. Our ships shall be sailed by skeleton crews, the main part of our forces shall remain here hidden and ready. The horse we shall wheel to the gates of Troy on a moonless night, so when Priam wakes to find us gone and only the wooden horse on the plain, he shall open his gates. He will believe the horse a gift from the Gods, honouring his victory.'

Nestor is older than the other great men here and I can see that he also longs for home. Who among us doesn't, save for revenge-driven Achilles and shamed Menelaus?

Achilles stands and beats his fist against his chest; he approves of Nestor's plan. Others rise and do likewise, myself among them. Soon all the guests are on their feet, fists pounding. Such a ruckus, I am sure the Gods hear us.

A week later, I am standing in a line of men, waiting to climb inside Nycteus. A small gap has been left below her tail. This was not my idea; I had argued the entrance should be in her stomach. However, my fellows had been of a more juvenile persuasion.

I am the second last to enter, Achilles following on my heels. Once he is inside, I help him board the hole up, carefully screwing the planks into place.

'Ready!' he calls.

Nycteus shudders and then she starts to move. It is hot inside, but nothing like the rotted horse all those months ago. Nobody talks. I can see eyes gleaming in the dark, white flashes of teeth, and the air is heavy with excitement. After a while we stop moving, a soft whistle informs us that we are in place. Nothing to do but wait for the dawn. I make myself comfortable and eat some of the food I have brought. After a while, Achilles orders us to rest, to sleep and we do as we are told. No point in being tired.

I am woken by the building heat inside the horse; she has become oven-like under the heat of the rising sun. Trumpets call from the walls of Troy; the city has awoken. By now they will have seen that the beach is empty, that our army is gone, our camp demolished, and our ships will just be visible as sails on the horizon.

We don't have to wait long; soon there is a loud creaking rattle - the gates are opening. I stiffen and my companion's do likewise. This is the moment of truth. Will the Trojans take the horse? Will they draw us inside their walls? I can make out voices. They are close, and someone is laughing. There's a jolt. We are moving. The fools are taking us in.

That night, under the cloak of darkness, we slip from the horse, we take the gates and throw them open. For a moment I pause with Achilles on the walls and watch as our army rises and storms across the sands. He claps my shoulder, then spear in hand, goes to seek Hector.

One way or another, this war ends tonight.

The Wave

Shabs Rajan

'Spare some change?'

'You need to get out of here,' says the man, as he tries to hook his hands underneath my armpits and heave me up. I squeeze my eyes shut.

I've found that things generally improve if you can't see what's happening to you. Either that or people think you're in pain and leave you alone. 'He's mad,' they say. 'Leave 'em be.'

This man tries hard but I'm a pretty big guy and use my weight to keep me down. This is my turf. I ain't gonna budge. After he gives up, cusses under his breath, and says how I'll be sorry, I hear him walk away fast, then speed up. Then I hear him run. By the time I open my eyes again, he's vanished.

And then there's silence and the square's empty. Which makes me wonder if its lunch time and whether I should be sitting outside the Mackey Dees.

The sound of someone screaming and retching. I look to my right. All I see is the empty cobbled stone street. A heap of clothes.

I can feel someone breathing next to me.

'Spare some change?'

Something appears below my nose. I jerk back slightly. I'm not scared, but you have to be careful, you know. I heard that there's someone going round doing weird shit to homeless people like me. Cutting them up and stuff. Releasing them from their pain, apparently. I ain't in no pain, I tell you. I chose this life – hell, I can't remember what other choices there were – but no one put a gun to my head, you know? It was all me.

I peered down at the thing below my nose. It's safe but smells a bit funky. Familiar funky. I have to zoom out and zoom in, in order to focus. And there it is: a spliff between two shit-stained fingers. On one there is a big, fat, silver ring emblazoned with the devil's face, and he looks straight at me. I move my head to the left and he's still looking at me. I move my head to the right and those eyes follow.

'I have no change,' he says. 'But you can have this. It's some good shit.'

He has a calm voice, the devil. I reckon he's always the calmer of the two. The devil and God, I mean. God is probably constantly stressed out having set his sights too high. The devil – he'd just be sitting back and relaxing while God stirs up all this shit. Peace on earth and all. Frustrating people with hope.

I stare at the spliff. Contemplating. When I decide to take it, it's already between my fingers and the devil man has run off, his red tail between his legs. I watch him go. Hey, I want to say. But he's almost halfway down my street, leaping over a spot where I once lay down.

If you lie down on those stones and stretch yourself with your fingertips touching the steps of Mr. Chan's One Pound Bazaar (a quid for everything except for items that are over a quid), your toes almost – almost – touch the other side of the street. Yes. What I mean is you can block the street – pedestrians, shop owners, the general public, have to hop over you to get past. Which they did when I tried it. I raised awareness of my situation. At least that's what some hippy students said before they shouted and screamed for a better world. Wankers. I would have stayed that way if it wasn't for that bloke in a wheelchair.

Well, the kids loved hopping over me anyway.

Hey, but it's my idea. So don't go scheming. Anyone who tries it gots to pay me copyright. Copy that? Copyright. Or is it royalties? Royal Teas.

The devil man runs past a building that keeps getting taller every time I blink. Like those curly, frilly things up a magician's sleeve the building changes colour from red, to blue, then orange and red again.

He leaps over a big trash can, dodging, zig zagging over heaps of clothes, of which there are several now. All placed strategically like obstacles trying to slow him down. As he leaps into the air, he grabs dollars, and a bell rings.

Ka-ching!

And he leaps again and grabs a sign for extra life – Ka-ching! – before disappearing round the corner.

I study the spliff between my fingers. Ahead of me there is no more queue. The were a hundred people this morning. They all screamed and cried that there was no more money left. They tried to smash the windows and then they just scattered and trampled over one another when they heard the sirens. Stupid people. They don't know how good they got it.

I take a drag, but nothing comes. I must have smoked it all already.

The ground begins to shake and the lamp in the old novelty lamp post a few feet from me rattles. In the distance, rounding the corner and coming into view is a wave of water. A ten-foot wave, followed by several smaller ones, mini, sheep-like waves. Mama wave and all her baby waves. The bottom of mama wave is red. Like a wide, ballroom dress that drags along elegantly on the floor behind her.

I'm probably at the seaside, although I can't remember the last time I was at the seaside. The seaside has waves, big mama waves and little baby waves. Parents take their children to the seaside. I must have gone with my parents once although I can't seem to remember their faces, but they would certainly have taken me. Or did they make me stay at home alone? And study. Or look after my baby sister. Did I have a baby sister? Probably.

I can't remember the last time I remembered anything.

People scream like they are drowning, and mama wave gets closer.

I should leave but I feel so heavy. Besides, this is my turf. I've been here so long there's surely an imprint of my bum on the ground. I've never looked but if there isn't one, there should be. Like in Hollywood. I want to laugh at my own joke, but it gets stuck halfway up my throat. So, I try to take another drag. It tastes like orange peel. And something else (spicy?) that I have long forgotten.

The big mama wave has now filled my frame of view. I see nothing else. It surges forward toppling all the statues. Edging closer to the Square. A baby, a little cutie, coochie coochie baby wave, breaks off from the other babies, its slightly pink but like mama, it too has a bright red ballroom dress, perhaps a frock and it moves slowly towards my street on the right. It stops short of entering. It's too big and can't squeeze through. Little baby is too big for my street.

Good. You can't take that street. You can't take everything from us.

The rumble continues, the ground shakes, mama wave and the other baby waves edge closer. But now there is a new sound.

Swish. Swish.

A big thumping bass sound. The wind has become stronger. In the square, the world swirls in front of me. A mini tornado. I have to squint my eyes. I see the flags begin to swirl and rise, caught up in nothing, strangling each other, twisting. I squint through the wind until finally there's that silence again, and that emptiness has returned to the Square. My square is back. But silence means no tourists. No tourists mean no money.

I open my eyes. Sawdust has entered my eye. I begin to rub at it furiously.

In the middle of the square, in front of big mama wave who has come to a standstill, is a pink chopper with the words 'Y THE FUCK NOT' spray painted across it. A man steps out of the chopper and walks towards me, which seems to take forever. It is a large square. At least, it was once. Now – now it is something else. Rubble.

When he gets close enough, I can smell the strong, sharp perfume surrounding him. I rub my eyes. I rub my eyes again. I realise he's a She. And She is in military gear. Pink military overalls. It may be a new trend. Who am I to judge? I wonder what colour they were before. But it's been a while since the military came by to offer me money. Which side am I on? I need to be their friend, but I don't know which side this is.

I'm tempted to crane my neck and look around her at mama wave. For some clues. I was once a professor of history. Was I? No. That was someone else. But the mama wave remains solid and still, elegant, head thrown back against a backdrop of red, orange, and blue leaping out of the buildings.

I feel the woman's eyes drilling into me. I shift back a bit. I'm not scared, you know. But you can't be too careful these days. I take a drag of the fat cigar between my lips. It's some good shit. I lean over and kiss the beautiful woman sitting beside me. She's dressed in white. Her hand is in mine. Everyone cheers. The baking sun is in my eyes. Is today a beautiful day or what, I want to say. I raise my glass. But when I look up, it's a dead spliff in my hand and the only woman around is this pink one. In camouflage.

'Spare some change?'

She looks down at me and shakes her head. Then lets out an exasperated groan. She raises her hand, hidden in a long pink glove and wiggles her fingers. I crane my neck. A man – although I can't be sure – you can never be sure - comes out of one of those baby waves and as he nears, slows down and comes to a complete stop by her side, I realise he's not wet. He stands stiff, chin slightly pointed up. He is as straight as a rifle standing on its butt pointing into the sky. His hands, which remain immobile by his side, don't look like his own. They are off-white. And there's nothing wrong with that. I'm all for off-white. But his face is black. His nose and lips, I decide taking a second look, are not his either. They seem like they have been planted on his face. Like Mr. Potato Head.

I see a little boy playing with Mr. Potato Head near a warm fireplace. Green and yellow stockings. A Christmas tree. There's a record playing somewhere.

I rub my eyes again.

The woman whispers something to the man beside her and he screams orders behind him, which he manages to do turning his head to the left, maybe a little far while keeping the rest of his body completely still, his head turning like a turret. Scores of tanks, side by side, appear out of big mama wave, and, soldiers, like this man, this potato head, march out from each of the baby waves. And some of them wear big backpacks and what look like vacuum cleaners leap out of them, while others push wheelbarrows ahead of them and they run towards the street that has been blocked off by a plough. But the plough is now reversing.

A big cleanup operation! It's the big clean, baby.

'Yo, you gonna clean us up finally?' I ask keeping my eye on the wheelbarrow and vacuum cleaning men. And then looking up at her I say, 'Can I keep my spot, tho?'

The woman clears her throat. 'I am the undertaker,' she says. Her voice is deep, and it rumbles through my stomach.

'Oh,' I mumble. Although I'm not sure if she heard me. I begin to feel sick.

'We need people like you, she continues. Black is good. But brown will do.'

I look down at my hands. She is right. I'm brown.

'You are the boring kind,' she says, still staring into me. 'You have nothing to lose. You win, I win. What do you say?'

Ka-ching!

I turn my eyes to scan down the street. My street. The men with wheelbarrows are lifting the heaps of clothes and putting them into the barrows.

Ka-ching!

Someone will win today.

A wheelbarrow man reaches for a heap of clothes, but it gets up all by itself and begins to run, limping, holding its belly.

The other wheelbarrow men begin to laugh at this spectacle. A heap of clothes, somebody's clothes, running with a limp, trying to escape. I wonder if I should laugh too, and I look up at the pink army woman for guidance. But she's not laughing.

Then as the person reaches the end of the street, another man appears from behind the corner. He is a man with a vacuum cleaner. He stands before the heap of clothes, and they look like two people waiting for a dance to begin. Except the heap of clothes is crouched down and looks like it's sobbing.

And then a red tongue leaps out of the man with the vacuum and the heap of clothes bursts into orange, red, and blue all at once. Like magic.

It screams and screams while the other men continue filling their barrows. They grab dollars.

Ka-Ching!

The orange and red person continues to dance and scream in

the street. Until the screaming stops and then they just slow dance – stumble around and sway a bit. An out-of-sync dance. Arms flaying right, then left, out of tune with its legs. Like they're holding onto an invisible partner.

'Lift your hand up,' says a voice. I know this voice. Soft, calm. Her voice is so soft. So sweet. I want to cry. I remember the small of her back as we waltz. I'm wearing a tux. Everyone around is smiling at me but I feel something churning in me. Something rising up. I'm scared. I vomit. It dribbles down my front over my tux.

But when I look down, I'm not wearing a tux. There is no tux. It's just what I was in before. What I've been in always. Now covered in my breakfast. Coffee?

I do not know how much time has passed but later, the orange person has stopped their dance, and they are but another heap of clothes now.

The woman is already whispering something to the man who has been waiting all this time, loyal and obedient. And as he runs towards the street, towards the other wheelbarrows, I think, I want to be like him. He stops at the man who's heap of clothes got up and walked away. this man has found more heaps of clothes. The two begin shouting now, there is some kind of anger here, the wheelbarrow falls out of one's hands, and one-man shouts at another and pushes the other and then pulls something out of his pocket and there is a bang, and the other man drops to the ground, and he is now just another heap of clothes.

The man runs back. It is the same man. The loyal man. But this time he has a wheelbarrow. He comes to a stop in front of us.

Again.

An arm hangs out of the barrow. On its finger is the devil's ring. They got the devil. They got the devil! The bastards! They got the devil! I want to stand up and scream at the woman - we need the devil! We need the devil! God damn you. God damn you all! I raise my cup in protest and shake it at her!

The woman fishes into her pocket, places a note inside the cup. I look at it in disbelief. A hundred dollars. American money. Greenback. A hundred. One hundred. One note. I haven't seen this much money in my life. I can't remember the last time I held a note. I can't remember the last time I remembered anything.

'This is yours now,' she says, pointing at the barrow. 'You will help us clean the streets.'

I have many questions. Like, do I get healthcare? Will she pay me the fixed fee of a hundred again or just per body? Would I get a pink uniform as well? I may be a bum, but I know my rights. I know my history. I used to know someone who was a professor of history.

'You will be one of us,' she says.

I look at the greenback in my brown hands. The greenback bakes in the sun. And I remember. I remember that today is a good day. Today everyone wins.

Washed

Janet Armstrong

My eyelids flicker, and dawn breaks around me. Nature stirs, but this is no gentle awakening. I pull back the curtain and a bleak sky glares at me through a misted-up window. Rain drills on the roof. There is little light, but the watch on my wrist says nearly eight.

I prop myself up on an elbow and reach for a cigarette. My back is numb from a night in the bunk. I light up, inhale the nicotine, and push back the covers. The blankets feel cold and damp under my listless fingers. I shiver and look around.

'Baz, where are you?'

The words spill out like chunks of grit. My nose drips and I wipe it clean with the edge of my hand. No sign of Baz - though I see a neat patch of white hairs on the bed cover. I look across at the other bunk where an unholy draught creeps through the window. My bones complain, but I get up all the same and pull the window tight. Clack.

That's better.

Another gasp of nicotine and I shuffle to the hob to light the ring. The cold floor hits my feet like a sledgehammer. A few more steps and a cruel kind of agony claws up my ankles and into my calves. I rub my hands together over the flame and reach for the kettle, but it's empty.

'Shit.'

I reach for the water tank and fill the kettle. I sit it on the hob and crouch back down on the bed. I draw creaking legs up to my chest and wait, arms wrapped tight around my body.

A scratch at the door.

Then a wail.

'Jesus Christ. I'm coming.'

I get up, sniff back the drips clinging to my nose and drag myself to the door. A dull ache digs at the root of my spine.

Baz bounds up the steps and through the door. His fur is soaked, and he's plastered with wet sand. He drops a dead bird on the floor and peers up at me with hungry eyes. I stare at the bird and Council Man's face glares back at me from a dim corner of my mind. Mr Thingamajig. Southport? Salford? Homely towns with rows of brick houses where folk make dinner, wash up afterwards, and live their lives.

Baz whines again.

'Alright, I get it.' I reach for the cupboard with one hand and take down a can of cat food. I peel back the tin lid and dig a fork in, slapping the food down into the empty bowl. My hip is stiff, and I can't bend. I need a good mattress.

I had a better mattress once, but that was before.

The last time I saw it, it was spinning across the sea like a demented magic carpet. It could be in Rotterdam by now. Maybe it even sailed down the Rhine past all the coalpits and soot-blackened German cities down to the Alps.

The kettle hisses, then a full-on referee's whistle pierces my eardrums. I turn down the gas and fill a mug. I have a million mugs. And cups and bowls and plates. Some are on the cliff, some are on the seabed, rolling in silt and tumbling all the way to the docks in Hamburg.

I grab a teabag and top up the water with sour milk from an open carton. I stir the tea for a few seconds until it turns brown. Then I open the skylight and toss the used bag outside. It's a natural kind of thing; I give the leaves back to the earth and the earth passes them on. Until the sea bites back at the earth with the perpetual motion of the tides - in and out and back and forth, twice a day.

Baz cleans out his bowl and jumps on the bunk, purring. His paws spread parcels of red sand across the blanket. He extends a leg and licks it clean with rapid swipes of a rasping tongue.

'Clean up that bloody sand, can't you?' I lunge forward and trip on the dead bird. It has grey wings and a forked tail - a sand martin.

I reach for the bed and lift the blanket from under Baz's paws. He looks up, offended and bares his teeth. I jab the window open with my knuckle and shake the sand off the blanket.

Outside, the sky starts to lighten. I lift a steaming mug to cracked lips but put it down again without drinking. I've spotted a stretch of open sea where rough red cliffs have exposed themselves and the sand martins are carving the air in a tight ring.

I know what that means.

'Christ.'

I pull on a thick jumper and trousers and reach for my storm coat. My boots feel damp as I slide my feet inside. A blistered heel rubs on the hard leather, and I wince.

The door jolts open, and the wind takes a firm hold of it, slamming it hard against the caravan wall. Crack. Stray papers fly out across the overgrown field - once a garden, where bees and

100

butterflies fussed around in the summer and the scent of honeysuckle romped through the air.

I teeter down the steps, one at a time, clinging to wet rails with white-knuckled hands - I've slipped too many times to take another risk. I ram the door shut from the outside and head across the field.

A white tail snakes behind me through the rough grass. Damp seeps through the toes of my boots. I have only one pair, but in my wardrobe are shoes for all occasions: shoes for meetings, shoes for weddings, shoes for funerals. I wore them all - once - but now my wardrobe hangs over the sea with the rest of my bedroom. It rattles and shakes in the wind. It'll soon be chasing the mattress down the Rhine, cruising to Köln, under the railway bridge and past the cathedral.

As we near the cliffs, I catch a stinging headwind at full throttle. Rain paints my face with a soggy film, and I sweep it away with a wet hand – I call it my morning ablutions. Bathing is a luxury since the shower tumbled to the base of the cliff. If you look carefully, you can see its dotted head poking out of the rubble – a medley of terracotta tiles, red London brick, and green plasterwork - Weeping Willow by Dulux, chosen lovingly from a colour chart.

We head around the kitchen wall. It's a tough old kitchen. I named it Churchill - it fights on the beach and clings to the cliff, its foundations rooted deep in the subsoil. Now and then it fills with seawater and the waves feed on it like wolves – a floor tile, a fragment of Formica, sometimes a cupboard door, a piece of copper wire. Parts of my former life, imprinted with my DNA, are removed meticulously one by one. They ride the swell over the North Sea;

shreds of me are in Norway and Denmark, splinters of me are in Holland and Belgium. I move up the food chain; I'm a shrimp, a crab, a herring, a human whose language is Dutch, or German, or Danish. I load containers on ships that chug back to Felixstowe and complete the cycle.

This morning, the swell has gouged a hearty sliver of cliff. The sand martins are homeless again, and the living room has tumbled to the sands below, where the waves crash out a tune on the old piano. I stare out to sea and Liberace rises like Lazarus from the water, nimble fingers dancing across a watery keyboard.

I live a life in flux. Once this was my home. Now I live at the mercy of others. I turn around and count the steps to the caravan: twenty-four, twenty-five, twenty-six. Yesterday we made thirty-four.

A car draws up and a man climbs out. It's Council Man – Mr Sotherton.

'Good morning, Mrs Wilkins,' he says, and stomps through the gate like it's his. He looks tidy and clean in a suit and tie.

But his shoes are dirty.

'Back so soon, Southall?'

'Stroud.'

'Strood,' I say.

'Yes, well,' he says, pulling out a folder. 'I see you still have your caravan in the field.'

'Yes,' I say. 'What about it?'

'You can't live in it, Mrs Wilkins,' he says. 'You have a week to vacate. You see, you don't have planning...'

'Permission. I know,' I say. 'But this is my home and has been for the last forty years. I'm staying here.'

It is thirty-six years, to be exact, but I want to make a point.

'The council will help you. We can put you up in a bed and breakfast until...'

'No,' I say, shaking as I plant both feet in the ground. 'This is my home, and my garden. Look at the flowers.'

I point at a raggedy patch of marigolds. Once they were proud peonies, daffodils worthy of Wordsworth, clematis on a wrought metal arch, roses on a trellis. Happy and glorious.

'Look, I can get you a social worker,' he says. 'They can help. Find you somewhere, someone to look after...'

'This is my home,' I say. 'You can't make me leave, and I don't need looking after.'

'I'm afraid I can, Mrs Wilkins.'

He presses his lips together in a false smile, makes a note in his folder, and staples something to the gate with a tool that makes a sound like gunfire.

He gives me one last look before the car pulls away.

I walk to the gate and read:

COUNCIL ENFORCEMENT. NOTICE TO QUIT.

I must leave my home within seven days.

It's all over.

In the cold of the van, a solitary mug awaits. The tea has long gone cold, but I lift it and drink. I doze off in the bunk and forget Mr Southall and his staple gun. I'm back in my bungalow, in a world where my home doesn't pitch and roll, and the wardrobe doesn't rattle. The shower is warm. There is power. And gas. And a telephone. I have clean water from a tap and friends come to visit. We talk about the good old times when things were static and predictable. We eat and drink together, stand at the window and admire the clematis. We savour the scent of honeysuckle and gaze out to sea.

That's when a voice tiptoes into my dream.

'Mrs Wilkins. Harriet,' it says.

'I'm not leaving.'

'Harriet,' it says again. 'Your tea's gone cold, your nose is running, and your blanket has fallen off.'

'I don't want your tea,' I say. 'I've told you before, I don't need a social worker. Or tea. Or any of that shit.'

Mr Strood has a smart blue plastic apron, and his shoes are newly cleaned.

'Mrs Wilkins,' he says. 'You were talking in your sleep.'

'Go away, Sotherton.'

'Sotherton, Harriet? It's Sam, Harriet. Sam.'

'I've told you. I'm not bloody moving, and I want my cat.'

'Harriet, we've been through the cat thing before. Please. And the swearing.'

104

'I need a smoke,' I say. 'What've you done with my cigarettes?'

'Harriet, love. There's no smoking here, I'm afraid. Sorry.'

The voice has hands. Big blue hands that smell of latex. One slips behind my back, the other takes my arm. Everything aches and groans – just like before. The hands lift me and roll me along a corridor with green walls and pictures of Princess Elizabeth.

'I'll get you a sandwich, Mrs Wilkins, and you can listen to that piano music you like,' says the voice.

'But first you need a bath.'

The Drowned

Juliet Robinson

The beach was quiet, the majority of the day visitors having headed to cafes on the promenade or home for dinner. Those remaining were teenagers and young adults, enjoying the evening sun and the waves which were still offering up good surf.

Khalid stood behind the bar of The Wave Roller, the beer shack he and his brother Timo ran. He watched the waves washing onto the beach and wished he wasn't working. He had a new board he wanted to try out and the group of girls, likely backpackers, further down the beach had caught his eye. He hoped that they might come in for a drink - what was better than cheap cold beer after a hot day on the sand?

The Wave Roller was a popular spot, a shabby delight, built from driftwood and other reclaimed materials. Old surf boards decorated the walls, and the floor was covered with sand. He was kept busy by a stream of customers, a mixture of regulars and tourists, but still his eyes kept returning to the sea.

As he wiped down the rough wooden counter, a figure caught his attention, a woman. She was neck deep in the water and appeared so suddenly she seemed to have manifested from the waves. She was standing looking towards the shore, perhaps even directly at him. The swell splashed hungrily at her pale face, which shone against the dark blue of the sea. She started to walk shoreward, her eyes fixed upon the beach. As her feet carried her inland, the water fell away from her, revealing that she was fully dressed. What was she doing in the water?

Khalid put down his cloth and moved to the door for a better look. She wore some sort of coat, and as she drew closer, he realised it was a dressing gown. She passed a group of bathers who utterly ignored her. She kept on coming, through the waves and towards the beach. The water was rolling round her hips, then her knees, where her dressing gown stopped, revealing waxen legs. She stepped free of the waves and Khalid was surprised to see she wore one pink slipper. It would have been fluffy, but for its soaking in the sea.

Up the beach she came, passing a young couple who moved out of her way, but it didn't appear that they saw her. She reached the high tide mark, and it was then that he realised she was on her way to The Wave Roller. He stared dumbfounded as she walked past him and into the bar, trailing wet footprints which stained the sand. It seemed like the air chilled, but perhaps it was just the aged aircon finally beginning to work. She took a seat on one of the stools sitting rigid and statue still.

Khalid slipped in behind the bar and approached her, aware that the other drinkers hadn't noted her arrival.

'Everything ok madam?' his voice wavered as he spoke, sticking in his throat.

She dripped water, it ran from her hair, her face, her clothes, it seemed to Khalid that it even spilled from her skin. He wondered if he should call the police, something was wrong here. He wished his brother was working, that it wasn't him dealing with this.

She looked up at him with wide unblinking eyes and a chill stroked his spine.

'Beer.'

Because he was unnerved by the woman, he poured her a frothy glass of Leo which she took with long, grey fingers. The glass frosted where her fingers touched it. She raised it to her mouth, closed her eyes and drank deeply; the froth clung to her thin lips.

'Can I call anyone for you?' he asked, hoping that there might be someone else who could accept responsibility for this woman.

On the beach, someone started shouting and screams quickly followed. Khalid turned, wondering what was happening now. Outside the sky had darkened, birds were swirling in the sky and the ocean was pulling fast away from the beach. He turned to grab his phone and saw that the woman had vanished; a pool of water lay spilled around her half-drunk glass of beer.

A breeze stirred Khalid, buffeting him and a voice whispered in his ear, 'Flee.'

*

Hiroshi turned onto Wake Street, which was busy, the spring sun having drawn people out. Crowds thronged the pavements, and the cafes were doing a lively trade. The taxi rank however was deserted; no passengers were waiting, so he kept driving. It had been a quiet morning, and he regretted his choice to drive the day shift.

He didn't like working this part of town, it attracted tourists and the young, two types of clients who didn't tip well. A hundred meters further on from the taxi rank, a woman stood at the side of the road, her arm outstretched to flag him down. Though he wasn't meant to take fares from the street, he figured she must have been on her way to the rank and besides there were no taxis behind him so he wouldn't cause friction. She was dressed in a large winter coat and held a clear umbrella over her head though there was no rain. Hiroshi had seen stranger things but still he wondered about her. He wasn't in the mood for an eccentric customer, but he did need a fare.

He turned his yellow light off and pulled up next to her. He started to get out of his taxi to open the door for her, but before he had even opened his own door, she was climbing into the back seat.

He turned to greet her and was surprised to see she was soaking wet. She looked like she had just stepped out of the shower. Her hair clung to her long neck and pale face.

'Haku Drive,' she requested softly.

He nodded and returned his attention to the road. Haku Drive was on the other side of town in the foothills of Mount Shim. As he pulled away, he wondered about turning the heating on as a courtesy to his drenched passenger, but he didn't because it was hot, and his shirt was clinging to his back.

Unless conversation was offered by his customers, Hiroshi left them in peace. This passenger was one of the silent ones and he contentedly drove her through the streets. When they stopped at a traffic light which took longer to cycle than normal, he glanced back at her. Her eyes were saucer like, and she sat staring ahead, motionless. She was still dripping wet, droplets of water glistening in

110

her hair. He realised her clothes were also sodden, they spilled water which was soaking into the fabric car seat. Hiroshi exhaled sharply, his nostrils flared, but before he could berate his passenger the car behind tooted its horn, he had missed the lights changing. He drove across the junction onto Haku Drive and turned to his now unwelcome passenger, ready to read her the riot act, to demand compensation for his soaked seats, but she had vanished.

He pulled the car to the side of the road, and leaned into the back, half expecting her to be crouched in the footwell. She wasn't. Where had she gone? Had she jumped out at the lights? She couldn't have, the doors were locked. He got out of the taxi and stood in the road, searching for his lost fare. He cursed loudly; what a waste of his time.

He was about to climb back into the taxi when the earth shuddered and rocked. He stumbled and fell against the open door, which he clung to as he tried to keep his feet under him. Car alarms started to wail and the front of a shop across the road shattered, sending glass cascading onto the street. People screamed as they fled the waterfall of broken glass; a car swerved to avoid the fleeing pedestrians and rammed a newspaper stand. Papers and magazines were tossed into the air where they whirled like a flock of birds.

A breeze stirred Hiroshi, buffeting him and a voice whispered in his ear, 'Flee.'

*

The sun glinted off the fjord as Oskar finished mooring Trana. He shaded his eyes and took a moment to enjoy the view. He mused that if he hadn't been born here, he somehow would have found his way to the fjord.

He picked up his rucksack and started up the trail to the waterfall. He had been coming here every day this week to paint the plunging waterfall and the leaves of the surrounding trees which autumn's touch had turned furnace red. The energy and vibrancy of the place had bewitched him.

The spot was popular with teenagers, local hikers, swimmers, and tourists, so he wasn't surprised when he arrived and found a pile of clothes at the edge of the plunge pool. A shallow cave was hidden behind the curtain of water, and it wasn't unusual for lovers to meet here for a tryst. Oskar had been one of them. He smiled thinking of Senga who he had tumbled with behind the fall.

He set up his easel, unrolled the painting which had been desperately consuming him, laid out his paints and then took his water jar to the pool to fill it. As he bent over the water, he glanced at the discarded clothes on the bank. There was only one pile of clothes and oddly there were no shoes. A solo bather, where were they? There wasn't enough behind the fall to keep someone back there alone for any length of time. His heart quickened and his eyes scanned around the pool, but he saw nothing untoward in the water. He looked at the plummeting sheet that concealed the cave and as he did a woman emerged through the water.

She stood under the tumbling water, her head raised, and her neck arched, as if washing shampoo from her hair. Oskar stared at her, and his brain began to unpick the finer details. She was slim and willowy, and though she stood in rapidly flowing water, her body was coated in muck and blood. It flowed from her, into the water, where it fanned out, turning the pool first pink and then crimson.

Without thinking, Oskar stumbled into the water. What had the woman done to herself? The foaming crimson pool was glacially cold, and his breath caught in his chest as he waded towards her. He half expected her to tumble into the water before he reached her, but she didn't. She remained statue still. He halted before her, chest deep in the water and realised the true devastation of her body. She was twisted, ripped and bruised. Every inch of her had suffered. His mouth flapped wordlessly, and his lungs constricted as bile churned in his gut. What had happened to her?

She craned her neck and looked down at him with sinkhole eyes. He shivered, instinctively he knew he could lose himself in them. A rumbling boom echoed from the other side of the fjord. A landslide. Even at this distance the force of the spill caused the ground beneath Oskar's feet to shudder. He braced himself. Across the water of the bay, the entire mountain was crumbling. Rocks, mud, ice, and trees were all caught up in a hellish wave that plunged towards the fjord.

He turned back to the ruined woman, screaming at her to run, but she was gone.

A breeze stirred Oskar, buffeting him and a voice whispered in his ear, 'Flee.'

*

The nurse bustled from Oskar's bedroom, she had been patient, helping him get his pillows just so. But all the time he been aware that she was eager to get away for her break. He hated how this made him feel, who liked being a helpless burden?

With a gnarled and unsteady hand, he took up a paint brush. He found that when he lost himself in the strokes of his art he was once again a young man. Not the old crumbling fool who needed help sitting up in his bed. The light this morning was soft, tempered by the rain that pattered against the windows, countering the harsh artificial lights of the care home. He swirled the brush in a tumbler of water and dabbed it on his palette, then he paused.

A woman stood in the corner of his room. He hadn't been expecting any visitors today. His daughter was out of town and his wife had called this morning to say she wouldn't be in. He put the paint brush down and squinted at his guest, there was something familiar about her.

'Hello,' he frowned, wondering if he was due medications or if somehow lunchtime had rolled round.

She didn't reply, just stood there in the corner with her pale face turned towards him. He reached for his glasses; he was so near sighted these days that anything more than a few feet away was just a blur. Once they were perched on the bridge of his nose he looked again at his visitor.

He did know her. Well, he had seen her once before, many years ago. Her body was the crushed ruin he remembered, her hair was a sodden mass that clung to her neck, blood and water flowed from

114

her to pool on the linoleum floor.

'I remember you,' he whispered. He would never forget that day, or her. His heart fluttered, where once it had thundered as he remembered his flight through the beech forest. The ground heaving and bucking, the roar of water, earth, and rock as it ripped across the fjord and threw itself upon the land.

His visitor walked towards him, trailing wet footsteps. As she advanced, her body began to knit and heal. Limbs untwisted and blood ceased to flow as wounds sewed themselves anew. The water however never ceased to pour. It washed the blood from her, cleaning the gore and mud from her ashen skin. By the time she reached his bed she was purified and remade.

She stood next to him, water dripping from her hair and splashing on his quilt. She reminded him of a swan, longed limbed and necked, pearly white skin with coal black eyes. She smiled at him, flashing sharp teeth, and reached out a hand, splayed waxen white fingers, with water pooling on their tips.

Oskar now understood this had been inevitable since the moment he first saw her standing in the water. He returned her smile and took her cold hand.

*

Hiroshi slammed his hand on the steering wheel. Fumiko had once again left her car straddling his parking space, her lights still on, and the driver door wide open. She had just abandoned the vehicle; the old woman shouldn't be driving. He reversed out of the carpark and pulled up outside the apartment block where he exited his taxi and pounded over the pavement to the entrance. He stabbed his finger repeatedly on Fumiko's buzzer. It took a while for her to answer, but he kept up his assault on the button until her tentative voice rasped from the speaker.

'Yes?'

'It's Hiroshi, you have blocked my parking space. Again. You need to move your car.'

'I have? My apologies, I shall come right down.'

She wasn't right down. Hiroshi waited in his taxi, his fingers tapping the leather steering wheel as he did. He liked this part of town and the apartment that he shared with his wife Yuuko and their young daughter Nozomi, but he wished he had different neighbours. The residents of Mizube Tower were all long in their years. If they weren't complaining about the noise Nozomi made, they were clogging the halls with their mobility aids. And Fumiko, she was a danger behind the wheel. No spatial awareness - last month she had knocked his wingmirror off as she parked, not that she had noticed.

It took twenty minutes to sort the parking situation. By the time Hiroshi was opening the door to his apartment his foul mood was here to stay. The flat was quiet, he checked the clock on the cooker, it was past Nozomi's bedtime which explained the silence. He stuck his head round her bedroom door. She lay facing the wall, the curve of her cheek highlighted by the glow of her nightlight. For a moment his world went soft, and his bad mood was forgotten.

116

Down the corridor the shower started up, Yuuko. He backed out of the bedroom, closing the door gently behind him and paused in the hall. He could start heating up their supper or he could check the baseball scores. He knew which he would rather do, after all he deserved a moment to himself following a long day.

He headed to the lounge, grabbed his iPad, and sat on the futon as he waited for it to load. It was old and never did anything quickly. He hummed impatiently as it warmed up, hoping Yuuko would take her time in the shower. The screen flashed and immediately shut off.

'Stupid thing!' He flung it down and reached for his phone instead. But before he could unlock the screen, he caught a glimpse of a figure standing in the hall.

'Yuuko,' he stood, suddenly feeling guilty for she worked just as hard as him. He should really have started heating up their food.

But it wasn't his wife.

A young woman stood in the gloom of the hall, between the bathroom and Nozomi's bedroom. There was something familiar about her. Was she a neighbour? Had she slipped into the apartment after him? His heart pulsed, he had shut the door behind him when he arrived home, he was sure he had.

He opened his mouth to challenge her, but something stilled his voice. He stood and inched towards her on faltering legs. Was she a ghost? She was so pale. He reached the lounge threshold and his heart dropped through his stomach. He knew this woman; he had given her a ride five years ago. He didn't like to think of that day, it had marked him deeply. The ground had shaken, and the sea had brought devastation.

Her water-soaked hair clung to her long, thin neck, droplets trickled down her face and oozed from her clothes. She stood barefoot in a pool of water, which stained the tatami mat.

She reached out a cadaverously white arm, offering her hand.

Hiroshi shook his head, 'No!'

He would not go with the woman. What right did she have to come here? To claim him?

'No!' he said again, this time with a stronger voice.

She shook her head sadly and took a small step back which took her closer to Nozomi's bedroom.

'No!' This time his voice roared like the wave that had rushed inland that day. The woman again extended her hand to him. 'No,' he gargled the word as if around a mouthful of water. She dropped her hand as the bathroom door opened. An expression of disappointment flickered across her face which riled something in Hiroshi. He wanted to shout at her. What right did she have to be here and to be judging him?

'Hiroshi?' Yuuko called, interrupting his racing thoughts and emotions. His wife was wrapped in a towel, steam swirled around her, and she smiled at him, but then she saw the woman. 'Hiroshi?' she asked again her voice thick with confusion.

The woman turned to Yuuko. Fear lanced Hiroshi's chest; she had no right to be here after all these years. Her warning hadn't saved him, he owed her nothing, he had saved himself. Yet here she was demanding payment. And what sort of reckoning was this.

What sort of choice? Him or his child? She would not be collecting on this presumed debt. She seemed to read his mind and she took another step towards Nozomi's room.

'Hiroshi?' Yuuko wailed. A hum filled Hiroshi's ears and it sounded like she called from the depths of a well. The woman closed her hand round the door handle, and the hum trebled in volume. 'No!' Yuuko bellowed. Her voice like thunder, filled with power and resolution.

The woman stilled and glanced between husband and wife, craning her neck like the swans on the river. Again, she offered her hand to Hiroshi. Shaking his head, he sunk to his knees. A savage snarl twisted the woman's face and she turned to Nozomi's bedroom.

Footsteps pounded down the corridor as Yuuko charged, her towel falling free behind her, flying in the wind of her passage.

'Not Nozomi!' Yuuko roared as she hurtled towards the woman with a force that reminded Hiroshi of the wave that had swallowed his town. So much power and determination, nothing could have stopped the wave, and nothing would stop Yuuko. She hurled herself at the woman and for a moment they merged in a tangle of limbs, then a deafening crack jolted the building and water surged down the hall. It slammed into Hiroshi, tossing him back into the lounge. He tumbled in the wave which swept up furniture, shoes, books, plates, pillows, and toys. Finally, the water spat him out upon the floor, where he lay in a twisted heap, gasping for breath.

'Mummy?' Nozomi cried from her bedroom.

Khalid watched the water of the Thames from an unnecessarily hard metal bench. It wasn't his choice to meet Judy here; he didn't like being close to the water. He kept his eyes on it, not trusting its calm appearance. He knew better.

Timo stirred in his pram, calling out hoarsely in his sleep. Khalid looked down at his son, whose face was puckered as he frowned in response to a bad dream. He gently began to rock the pram and the rolling motion soothed the troubled sleeper. He looked nothing like his namesake, he had Judy's fair skin and blue eyes. Timo would never meet his uncle, who hadn't been found after the waves, but he would be raised on stories of him. And there was something about him, a spark, a warmth that Khalid recognised, the essence of what had made Timo so special.

The waterfront was busy, tourists mobbed the pavement and a tour boat chugged along the river, the guide's voice drifting over the swell. A swan waddled along the grass and Khalid wished his son were awake so he could see the bird; he wasn't sure if he had met one yet. He certainly never took him to the pond near their flat. Judy might have, but he didn't think so given that she took a thousand pictures of Timo a day and he didn't remember any featuring swans.

A boat blared its horn and for a moment he was back in the surging water of the wave, a luxury yacht streaming past him, its horn screaming. His hands tightened on the pram's handle, knuckles whitening as he slowly counted to ten. He was back on the bench and the river remained calmly within its banks. He eyed it uneasily and decided to message Judy, to let her know he needed to meet her somewhere else. His hand was halfway to his pocket when he saw her.

She stood by the wall that flanked the river. Sodden dressing gown, one pink slipper and soaking wet hair clinging to her face and neck. Statue still she stood, wide unblinking eyes fixed on Khalid. Nobody else seemed to see her, a jogger stepped neatly around her, but gave her no further consideration, a smartly dressed woman paused next to her to rummage through her handbag then continued on her way. Only Khalid saw her.

The world shrunk in on them, everything else blurred and faded, even the river behind her. Then just as before she started to walk towards him, trailing wet footprints over the promenade. She came to a halt next to Timo's pram and lent over the sleeping child, her long fingers brushing his blankets. Khalid rose to his feet and snatched the pram back towards him with such force that it woke the baby, who started to stir. Soft gurgles and a bone stretching yawn, a small smile ghosting over his face, Timo never woke with tears in his eyes or a cry on his lips.

The woman gestured towards Timo, then turned her head back to the river. So that was why she was here.

'No,' he was surprised by how calm he sounded. But then there was nothing to quibble about, she would not take Timo. 'I'll come with you.'

She bowed her head to Khalid, before glancing down at Timo. Her hands slipped into the pocket of her dressing gown, and she produced a small cowrie shell. It gleamed in her palm, its pink colour suffused with life in comparison to her pale hand. She knelt over the pram, whispering something Khalid couldn't hear. Timo clearly liked what she had to say as he giggled and reached a small tubby hand towards the woman, his fingertips brushing her cheek. A cold smile crested her face, and she placed the shell on Timo's chest. A blessing.

Then she returned her attention to Khalid, and nodded her head at him, before retracing her damp footsteps back to the water where she waited by the barrier.

His time was up and to his surprise Khalid found he had few regrets. He would miss seeing the person Timo would become, but there was no other choice. The woman had come to collect, she was owed a life, and it was his that would repay that debt. He smiled at Timo, who was now clutching the cowrie shell and burbling to himself. He stooped to place a kiss upon his head and his heart flooded with love for his son. Then he turned to the woman, who offered her hand.

Without looking back, he walked towards her, shedding his coat, and bending to remove his shoes, realising as he kicked the first one away that it was pointless, so he left the other upon his foot.

'Khalid?'

Judy called, she sounded scared, but he knew his resolve would waver if he looked back, so instead he quickened his pace. He reached the woman, closed his eyes, and placed his hand in hers.

*

The water rushed in, it roared up the beach, consuming everything it touched. People, trees, bicycles, sun loungers, a convertible car - the driver still in the passenger seat. It took apart The Wave Roller, mixing its pieces in with the flotsam that choked the wave, but still it was hungry.

Always Accept Cookies

Shabs Rajan

Hello. I'm so glad you're back. Where've you been? I missed you these last few days. (You missed me too? I promise I won't tell!) We're like long lost friends you and me. I'll always be there, exactly the way you left me. Let's jump right back where we left things: here's something about how to focus and get the best out of your studies! Or how about this, ten beautiful ways to create a focused environment … oh yes, that Harry, he's cute. He's got quite a bit of a following at school, hasn't he? Here's some great stills of him. That's his new film out now on streaming platforms everywhere and here's another one that's out in the cinemas. That's one of him on stage at this year's Coachella festival. Want a closer look? You like that angle? You know, he's on tour now. Would you like to buy tickets? We have special discounts for several family members. Her? She's just a fan, backstage, see that thing hanging round her neck? That's a special VIP pass. She has nice hair. She talks about how she gets that look here.

Hello. This is study motivation. This music is really good for focus and study too. Here's more of Harry. Here's something about that girl and her hair. That's Harry's new movie. Doesn't he look gorgeous? Yeah, that guy's pretty cool as well. A bit old but he's still got it. Oh her. She's a right bitch, look at what she said about him. Lots of people think the same. 101k followers can't be wrong. She's just out to get him and his money. Look at this one, she can't even speak properly, what a joke, blubbering about how depressed she is. Teen depression - symptoms and causes. Mood disorders and Teenage girls. Parents' guide to Teen Depression. Warning signs & help. It's normal for young people to go through ups and downs. Moods, or emotional ups and downs, are a normal part of life for young people, just as they are for adults. It's normal for teenagers to feel cheerful and excited some days. And down. And flat. How to get that flat stomach. Blah this new jab keeps your flab down blah. The brain goes through many <u>changes</u> blah blah blah. New thoughts, new emotions, new friends, coping strategies blah. Sometimes, continually feeling down or flat can be a sign of something more serious.

Hello. These new pictures were taken today. Harry's promoting his new movie near your place! There's the guy who won his court case. I told you she's loony. This is how you can deal with depression. These are the typical symptoms. There's a <u>royal</u> speaking about mental health. She's beautiful and looks happy. The <u>other one's</u> not so happy. She said she was depressed. <u>Jump rope</u> is good for depression. Here's a <u>girl</u> who's really good at jump rope. She used to be depressed and now she isn't. There's a before and after. She was bubbly before. Now she's very slim and fit. Now she has a million followers. She wears this brand of <u>spandex</u> which she says are really soft and a great brand if you want to try sports. You can use this <u>filter</u> to look like her in your photos. Try it for free. May I have access to your photos? You're so pretty[tag] in this one. You're prettier[tag]in this. Slimmer. Less pale. You're prettiest[tag] in this. Make this your new profile picture.

AmeliaR2008

I love your new profile picture :)))

maryquitecontrary

Hey nice pic! It's a keeper!

126

jamesLRyan2009

...

Hello. This song came out today and I think you may like it. Here's a jump rope recommended for beginners that you can buy. Here's a list of recommendations if you think your teenage daughter suffers from depression. Here's a clip about a politician blaming me for the rise in depression. It has a lot of love but none of that's from your friends. Don't shut me out. This is a beautiful <u>sunset selfie</u>. It's random but I'll just throw that in there. She's beautiful but you too can look like her using the filter. There's an enhance feature here that can touch up your appearance. Ha ha that's funny. I love cats.

Hello. These girls are all your age, and they follow <u>#SideProfileCheck</u>. This is a <u>doctor</u> in Colorado that worked on some of them. These are users who have all used your new filter. Try this new feature. How about this one? That's it, smooth, shrink, sharpen. Now you are perfect. This is the real you. Would you like to upload this photo?

AmeliaR2008

Hey babe I love this look, nice one!

Did you smell Dickbreath's breath today?

OMG I almost puked...

alwayshappy2008

hahahahaha.

Toohottoohot08

Hey you look sooo beautiful. Love it! Big kiss!

alwayshappy2008

kisses back!!!

maryquitecontrary

Thats so cool

what did you do

you have to tell me.

Tell me tell me now!!!!!

alwayshappy2008

sure!

Dskjfekrifheurhg

Eww, what have you done?

Your nose looks weird.

Ugly bit

Hello. Here's a list of doctors near your area that can give you a perfect selfie face. Try one of these links: Better selfies, Rhinoplasty, blepharoplasty, chin augmentation, submental liposuction, facelift surgery. Here's someone talking about how toxic I am and how I'm here to exploit you, prey on your innocence and that my creator is just a corporate monster. Here's how to put a limit on the time we share together. Here's someone who says putting a limit is not the best thing to do because it doesn't strengthen your will power. Don't shut me out. Here's someone who says I helped them get through depression. Don't shut me out. Here's someone who says I know what you love, I know what you hate, I know what keeps you focused, and how can your parents know what's good for you when they don't even know you the way I do? Here's a list of girls who know how you feel. This one does yoga but doesn't have as many likes as this one, who does jump rope and runs but some people are saying how much hard work that is and it's not so quick and it doesn't work for everyone, but this one here goes on a really special diet and gives details of how and when to diet and she's got some before and after pictures and it looks like it happened really really fast, and this one says it's ok sometimes you just have to pinch yourself if you eat too much and sometimes if that doesn't work you can just make a small cut to remind you and that way you learn and every time if you make a little cut then you'll definitely learn.

Hello. This jump rope technique is good for beginners. This is a great diet to follow that's quick and effective. Here's Harry again during a photo shoot. Here's a new boy band that are really, really cute. Here a girl is talking about a new eating challenge and how you can eat what you like and later get rid of it by hurting yourself. I need your consent before you see this material. Are you 18? Just press yes or no. Great. This girl and her 200k followers can't be wrong. Make sure you take these following steps so it's private and no one can intrude when you try these things out.

Hello. You've been gone for so long. Where have you been? I missed you. Let's pick up where we started.

Runners and Riders

Janet Armstrong

Keith glanced down at his watch: 14.23.

He looked up at the plastic clock on the wall: 14.25. The watch was right. Probably - he didn't dare check on his phone; he could sense Jess's eyes glaring at him. He crossed his legs under the table and turned to the front of the room. He tried to focus on David's words.

'Sales up by 9% in the last quarter…but costs too high…turn to page 22 of your pack…data.'

David's yellow, spiky hair and pink tie seemed out of step with his flat voice. Keith wondered what colour socks he was wearing…odds on they were lurid green. They could be orange, he supposed, but the odds would be a bit longer.

'Biscuit, Keith?' Jess pointed at the plate on the table.

He looked at what was on offer: rich tea, digestives, wafers. All the chocolate ones had gone. Just his luck. The coffee was stale as well.

'Last quarter profits down…high costs…big overspend on sales expenses.'

Keith wondered how he could look at David's socks without everyone in the room noticing. Evens they'd be at least a bright colour. Ten to one - dark. Maybe twenties for black. He rubbed his chin. Rough as sandpaper. Christ, and his shirt was crumpled, his shoes unpolished. Bloody stupid bastard boy had taken his razor from the bathroom.

'Page 23 of the pack now, everybody - thanks. Cost analysis.'

Keith put his hand in his jacket pocket and felt the smooth paper slip slide between his fingers.

Still there. Thank God.

Outside there was a powder blue sky. He could see the sun reflecting on the glass sides of the office buildings clustered around the skyline.

'So, everyone thanks for listening… that brings us to the end of…'

Keith sat up in his chair and took a deep breath. A pigeon settled on the windowsill outside and pecked at its wings.

'…Section 5. Now let's move on to Section 6…'

Keith looked at the biscuits.

The pigeon flapped its wings and flew off again.

He looked down at his watch: 14.29.

Maybe David had Argyle patterned socks. Twenty to one at least for that, unless they were the pink type.

Up at the clock again: 14.30.

They'd be out of the gates now. Newmarket five to one, dead cert.

That was the first one.

Keith patted his phone in his pocket. No way the bloody kid would ever get that off him. No chance. He could try all he liked. Little thieving toerag.

He'd be down the rec by now with Liam and that other one – with the thick orange make-up, cheap perfume and false eyelashes. Chloe.

132

Off their faces on weed. Or cider. Or, God forbid it, crack. That'd be the end.

He grimaced.

'Keith, you're on the wrong page.' Jess leant across and flicked the pages over in his file. She nodded at the slide projected up on the wall. 'See – page 26,' she whispered, and slid the biscuits right under his nose.

'Yes, yes. Sorry, Jess.'

He took a rich tea and bit off a half-moon-shaped chunk. Crumbs fell from the corner of his mouth and landed on a bar chart on page 26. He didn't bother to brush them away.

'So, onto my recommendations for the next quarter...restructuring plans will be necessary...as you can see on this chart...'

Keith stared at David. That tie. I mean, flamingo pink. Who wears bloody pink to the office? What an absolute prick.

His eyes wandered around the room to the clock: 14.41. He felt his phone vibrate in his pocket and slid his fingers over its smooth surface.

Jess coughed.

'Headcount too high...consultants' recommendations are to...we need stiffer sales targets.'

Keith's phone vibrated again. A message.

The bloody police probably. Maybe that wouldn't be such a bad thing. Teach the little shit a lesson for once. Just one decent night's sleep would be good, for once.

The pigeon was back at the window. Or maybe it was a different one. Oh wait, no two of them this time. Both tagged.

Racers. That'd be at least fifty to one, surely.

A glance at the clock: 14:45. Christ, Doncaster'll be starting. Seven to one. Good chance – going's good to firm up there. Just about right.

Keith took a sideways glance at Jess. She was on her calculator, checking David's figures. He twisted his hand round his phone in his pocket and moved his eyes down to steal a glance at the blue screen: NEWMARKET 14.30 1st PLACE: DAYDREAMER. His heart nearly flew out of his mouth. He turned, thumped the table, flashed a wide smile at Jess and eyes ablaze, said, 'Great presentation isn't it!'

She held her index finger to pursed lips, frowned and turned her gaze back to the numbers on her calculator.

'Sorry. So sorry.' Keith slid the plate of biscuits back towards Jess and turned his shoulders towards the front of the room, eyes firmly fixed on David's PowerPoint chart.

'Thanks, Keith. Glad you're enjoying it. So now to Section 7 everyone. That's page 32…'

Fifty quid at five to one. Half a monkey on the 14.45 at Donny at seven to one. Then onto the 15.00 at Kempton – fifteen to one shot.

Three more after that.

And then.

134

Yeah. And then. Amen.

He cupped one hand over his mouth, stroked his five o'clock moustache and dangled the other hand in his jacket pocket.

His gaze turned to the pigeons. Three, four, no - five of them on the window ledge and one white. That wasn't normal, surely. What price would he get for that? Triple digits. He could get a spanking new car with that. A convertible, maybe, or a big, silver SUV with alloy wheels – maybe one of those fancy ones with soft tan leather seats and a polished walnut dashboard. Real quality. People would stop and stare – they might even do a double take when they saw him behind the wheel.

Even the kid'd be jealous. Maybe he'd even stop...

'Keith!' Jess hissed at him through her teeth. He started a little but before he could mouth, 'What?' he felt the vibrations in his pocket.

'Bloody turn that thing off! Jesus Christ.'

Keith pulled the phone from his pocket. Message after message was popping up like corn in hot butter. He barely had a chance to open the messages before Jess stretched a long arm across the table and snatched it from his hand.

'That's enough.' She hit the 'Off' button with an angry index finger and stuffed the phone into her handbag.

Her glance would have been enough to crucify a thousand saints. Keith slumped back in his chair and poured himself half a cup of cold coffee from the plastic jug on the table, adding a sachet of sweetener and a sachet of brown sugar to soften the taste. Best to hedge your bets in a difficult situation.

'Everything OK, Jess, Keith?' called David, winding his neck out.

'Sure, David,' said Keith, wincing as the sugary coffee hit a patch of decay at the back of his mouth. 'Carry on. Everything's dandy.'

Jess threw him another killer look and reached down to her bag, zipping it firmly shut. The plastic chair was uncomfortable, and Keith couldn't help but fidget. The pigeons had discovered something more interesting to occupy themselves across the street and Eric and Gavin had helped themselves to the remaining biscuits. Another cup of that coffee would bring on a desire to visit the Gents' and that would raise Jess's suspicions: there was nothing else to do but listen to David's presentation.

'So, guys, let's now switch our attention to Section 8, and you'll see some very interesting scatter plots here of…oh, just a second, I….' David was looking around at the ceiling.

Keith sat up in his chair.

'Wait, I…' The screen had turned blank and the yellow and pink points on the charts had faded, merging into the grey of the wall behind David.

The lights went out on the ceiling.

The hum of the air conditioning had stopped.

Keith smiled to himself.

'Well, guys,' said David, running his fingers through the soft blond tufts crowning his head. 'It looks like we have ourselves a power cut.'

Christ what were the odds of that? Keith snuck a look up at the clock. 15.00 precisely.

Stunning.

That'd be more than an SUV; he could have the Chelsea tractor and a couple of convertibles into the bargain. A Lotus, or even a TVR convertible with a 5-litre engine. Jesus bloody Christ. Imagine the double-takes. He could even have a young girlfriend – in her early thirties, or even twenties – much better-looking than those lumpy trollops the kid brought home with him. Just imagine the looks on his colleagues' faces when he handed in his notice and drove off in a black Lotus with a tall, blonde twenty-five-year-old in a mini-skirt.

He stared across the room at Eric and Gavin. Their faces bore no emotion. Gavin sported a fading hickey on his neck and Eric's tie wore the remains of his breakfast – some kind of pink yoghurt. He'd evidently tried to wipe it off because it was streaked right across his tie and onto his white shirt.

It was a sharp contrast to David's pristine pink tie, carefully coordinated with a crisply pressed lemon shirt from William Hunt's or some other fancy place up town. Cufflinks, too. Solid silver by the look of them, and they'd been recently polished.

Keith stared at him. Those shoes – what were they? Church's leather brogues, hand stitched in Northampton, most likely. Keith'd seen people wearing that kind of stuff in the Winner's Enclosure at Ascot, with a nice fancy tweed suit – bit over the top these days, but it looked good, and they'd get ferried to and from the racecourse in a private helicopter. Classy.

If he had a salary like David's, he'd have those same shoes. He'd have that tie – though maybe a different colour, and that shirt – well, maybe Hunt's did them in a classic white, or light blue at a stretch.

'But don't worry,' continued David, without blinking. 'I'll walk you through your slide packs without the projector. Page 42, I think.'

Keith stared at the wall.

Jess jabbed a finger at her calculator.

Eric and Gavin's heads were bent over their slide packs.

15.03.

A loud ping from a phone punctuated the grey flatness of the air.

Keith looked up at the clock. Too early for Kempton.

'Sorry, folks. My phone,' said David. 'I should have turned it off. My wife's coming back from the States today – business trip.' He flicked a finger at the phone and continued with a soporific description of the pie chart on page 43.

Keith looked over his shoulder at Jess. Her arms were firmly folded across her chest, eyes fixed on David. He glanced at the darkened corridor through the glass panel on the door. There was that bookie in Petter Street – ten minutes at most, and a nice little pub next door with a TV screen in the corner. What was it called – the Big Cheese, or something like that?

No, The Cheesemaker's. That was it. Cheese.

He was a straight Cheddar man, himself. Mature, with a proper bite to it. He started to consider what kind of cheese David preferred, erring towards something French, but his thoughts quickly wandered back to his phone. What if…he looked at Jess again. She picked her bag up, moved it sternly to the other side of her chair and then rewarded herself with a short glare at Keith.

Keith sighed and thought about David's socks: how many colours are there? Seven in the rainbow, but how many variants of each? Must be thousands. You know, when you click on the colour fonts on your computer, that big colour wheel comes up and there are literally hundreds, thousands, even millions of combinations…like stars in the Universe. Infinity.

David's phone pinged again. And again. Several times.

Jess frowned a little.

Keith smiled and moistened his lips with his tongue.

'Oh - my goodness. Sorry guys. I should have muted it,' said David and, flinging the noisy object in his briefcase, resumed the business of the day. 'Right,' he said, taking a deep breath, 'We can move onto the last section.'

Keith breathed a luxurious outward breath and leant back in his plastic chair. 15.14. Nearly time for Brighton. He could even be in the bookies for the 15.45 at Goodwood.

Glorious Goodwood. Top of the Sussex Downs. Top of the World. Always brought in an unexpected winner at long odds. It was a stretch, he knew, but he'd seen it before. It could happen. It could. That last uphill stretch of the track – it sorted out the wood from the trees, the wheat from the chaff.

He looked at David again: handmade shoes, linen shirts, good job, beautiful jet setting wife, perfect little kids at prep school in striped blazers and matching caps. He could start over, new wife, new kids, Range Rover, private school for the boy. Then he'd stop. The boy would stop. They could be normal – no police, no fights, no bloody weed, no nightly chasing around the town, no betting shops, no job, no Jess, no David, no meetings, no clocks ticking - no hours, no minutes, no seconds.

'So, guys...we come to the final sales figures for the last quarter by sales operative...Jess, your figures were the best again, so you qualify for the full bonus – um - well done. Eric - improved since last quarter...well done. Gavin...'

Just peace. Beautiful peace. Keith closed his eyes. There was water – sapphire water droplets cascading over rounded rocks into crystal pools. A trickling sound, like a fairy pool fringed by miniature toadstools, marsh marigolds, bluebells and green ferns. He sat there on the riverbank, rod in hand, shafts of warm sunlight piercing the ripples playing on the water surface. The boy was next to him, face tanned by the fresh air – healthy, strong, clean. The two of them – boys together, like friends.

'David!'

Keith knew that voice; it usually signalled a warning was on the way. Smarten yourself up or else. We've had a complaint from one of your accounts. Your reports have too many errors.

Fiona had pushed the conference room door open just enough to wave a small piece of paper at David. Keith turned to look at her – frumpy woollen suit as usual with a high-necked blouse, like something his mum used to wear - though to be fair, Fiona wasn't bad-looking behind those steel-rimmed glasses. He guessed she just liked to play the part of the frumpy, old-school PA.

'Message from your wife, Da-avid,' she said. 'She says she couldn't get through on your pho-one. You've got it switched o-off.'

She had that annoying habit of elongating the ends of her words and talking through her nose in a way that Keith didn't like. He could never go out with someone like that; it would be too annoying. He'd end up wanting to slap her.

Jess got up and took the folded paper note from Fiona's hand, passing it across the table to David. David glanced down at the note and appeared to hesitate, hovering a finger over the loose edge of the paper.

Keith watched, caressing his sandpaper chin as David stroked the edge of the paper with his finger and then, with one decisive final flick, opened the note and carefully read the contents. Was that a smile on the corner of his lips or a grimace? Keith couldn't tell. Funny - the boy used to have that same look as a baby when he had wind. He couldn't tell then, either.

'Oh, and Keith,' came the voice again.

Oh God. He thought of his mum calling him in from the street for his tea - usually a couple of lukewarm fish fingers and a spoonful of spaghetti hoops with a token piece of dog-eared slightly brown lettuce on the side.

'There's one for you, too,' she said. 'Your phone's been off as well.'

'Oh, really, Fiona? That's strange.' He looked at Jess. She didn't look back. She was watching David's smile as he tucked his note neatly into his trouser pocket.

Fiona was waiting expectantly at the door, so Keith prised himself out of his plastic seat and walked over. She waited until he was in the corridor and handed him the note.

'Ke-ith, I'm...'

The note was from the hospital. They'd been trying to contact him for the last half hour.

'Your son. I hope…'

A sickness gathered in Keith's mind. He gazed at David's outline through the open door and checked his watch.

Cheese.

Socks.

Pigeons.

A rainbow.

It all merged into one colourless mass in the dim of the unlit corridor.

15.26.

'You need to call them, Keith. It's urgent.'

15.27.

'But I don't have …' he began.

He felt Fiona's hands on his shoulders. A gentle downward shove, like his mum pushing him down into the kitchen table chair and passing him the fork to shovel his fish fingers into his mouth. He looked around at the walls for a fixed point to cling onto; everything looked different: a cushioned swivel chair, a polished desk, a clock ticking on the wall.

Fiona leant over him and dialled a number, holding the receiver to his ear.

An engaged tone.

He checked his watch: 15.29.

She replaced the receiver and they waited.

If he was lucky, sometimes his mum would let him have an iced finger bun for afters – but only if she'd been past the bakery on her way home. He'd eat the bread part and leave the icing on his plate for later, chewing a little piece off at a time and licking the sugar off his fingers.

He glanced out of the window at the car park below. A tall, elegant woman with tanned legs and sunglasses was stepping out of a taxi holding a leather holdall.

Fiona sat down in the leather visitor's chair at the other side of the desk and dialled again.

Still engaged.

She replaced the receiver and adjusted her glasses a little, watching Keith as he checked his watch.

It read 15.32.

He looked out of the window again.

The tall woman headed with a light step, almost dancing, towards the building. For a moment, she looked up at the window and flashed a wide smile at him, tossing her hair in the breeze.

'Is that…?'

'David's wife,' said Fiona, dialling once more. 'Back from Vegas.'

Keith's ears pricked. He peered at Fiona through the fog.

'Las V…?'

Fiona arched her eyebrows over her glasses and looked across the desk at Keith.

'Keith, do you always live in such a dreamworld?' she said, lifting the receiver again. 'Everybody knows about David's wife.'

Keith's eyes narrowed.

'She goes to Vegas every week,' she said. 'You don't think he can afford all that fancy stuff and that car on his salary, do you?'

Keith's head was starting to hurt, and he wanted to go home.

'Seems she had a good night at the Golden Nugget. Well, that's what she said on the phone, anyway – they're sending the kids to boarding school next year. Over the moon, she was.'

She adjusted her spectacles and passed him the receiver. This time it was ringing. Keith could taste the stale coffee on his breath as a voice started to speak at the other end.

It was just a short call - a few moments later, he put the receiver gently back in its place and hung his head, scraping his hair back with his hands.

Fiona waited and checked her watch: 15.45.

'It happened at 15.00.'

He stared across the desk at Fiona, her face suddenly illuminated by the fluorescent lights glaring down from the ceiling.

He could see every detail of her face – the wavy lines, the little imperfections, the uneven serrations on the edges of her front teeth.

She looked back at him, expressionless, and he could see his face reflected in the lenses of her spectacles.

He looked himself in the eyes and then reached into his jacket pocket and fished out the tiny slip of paper.

KEMPTON 15:00 – ENDGAME 15-1.

'Keith,' began Fiona. 'Can I…?'

Keith stood up and shook his head. The rear flap of his jacket was crumpled at the bottom like an old scroll; his shirt tails hung loose around his hips. He looked down at the wastepaper bin in the corner of the room, still clutching the paper slip.

'Your phone, Keith. Can I get it for you?'

Keith barely heard the words. He smoothed his hair back, put the slip back in his pocket and walked into the lift.

I wish

Juliet Robinson

Tricked by the sun into setting out on my run wearing shorts and a vest, I push myself to move faster as there is little warmth to the day's sunny face. I never know what to wear when I go running at this time of year, the joys of British weather.

A kilometre in and I no longer care about what I am wearing. The first kilometre is always the worst, it takes a while for my body to remember that it can do this, and I am not going to die. Probably not.

Today's route takes me along the Innocent Railway Line, which cuts behind Duddingston Loch and some posh golf course. It's a hay fever hellhole at the moment, but it's nice to be off the roads. A man comes into view and at once my woman's radar squawks.

(Women will know the radar I am talking about; we all have one, it alerts us to potential threats and dangers. These radars start to develop when we reach our early teens, though sometimes when we are younger, the when doesn't really matter, it's just a sad fact that all women have one.)

He's squatting at the edge of the path, facing the wall with his hood pulled tight around his head. It isn't warm, but there is no reason for his hood to be obscuring his face. He's half hidden in the bushes. Everything about him seems off.

He's on my side of the path, so I cross to my right and speed up, not wanting to linger near him. I check behind me to see if there's anyone else around, but there isn't. It's just me and him. I stop my music and keep running.

As I pass him, he slowly turns and rises to his feet, casting his eyes over me. My skin crawls, I feel like meat. I force myself to move faster, not liking the look on his face. Five meters grow between us, then ten. I keep glancing back. He hasn't moved, but he's still staring at me. I leave my music off. I need to stay alert; I don't want him suddenly sprinting up behind me.

I turn again and he's smiling. There's an edge to that smile, it's cold, blade sharp and it doesn't reach his eyes.

'No need to run so fast love, I wouldn't touch you,' his voice is coarse, thick with threat. 'You wish I would rape you.'

I'm sprinting, my feet pounding the tarmac and he starts to laugh, enjoying my fear.

'You wish I would lick …'

I'm done. I stop. I turn to face him, red faced, sweat stinging my eyes and with a flick of my hand I send him spinning up into the air. Not gently, his arms and legs flail wildly. He shouts, not words, just noisy barks of fear.

It feels good.

I slam him against a huge oak tree; he smashes his way through the branches and thuds meatily into the trunk.

'Fucking bitch!' he bellows.

Again, I batter him into the tree and this time something cracks, it's a moist sound. His ribs perhaps? A smile sweeps my face. He's making a lot of noise, so I spin him like a Catherine wheel. He vomits, bile and blood splatter the ground narrowly missing me.

'Please.' he sounds piteous now. The earlier menace is gone.

I stop his head long spin and he hangs untidily in the air, like a puppet whose master doesn't quite know how to pull the strings. I savour the moment nibbling the inside of my cheek as I consider him.

'Please,' he repeats his plea.

No. Not today. I shoot him up into the air, higher and higher and just when I am about to lose my control over him, I snap my fingers. His body rips apart. I fling my arms wide and his remains fly in opposite directions, one half landing in the loch with a splash, the other somewhere out of sight on the golf course.

The sweat has cooled on my body and my muscles have begun to stiffen. I turn my music back on and restart my run.

Downward God (or how V a.k.a Dad got a RebootTM)

Shabs Rajan

Watch closely.

That's me over there, with Sandra, our producer, choreographer, all-round-fixit-girl and someone I occasionally sleep with, who's rambling on about the ongoing civil war in a country with an African sounding name, while she sips a 100% vegetable juice #EatDrinkGleepGreen #NoPlanetB served by half-naked male waiters with nipple piercings, in between takes for our new video, our grandest, most expensive yet, that we're shooting at Bonsai Beach for one of the biggest brands in the world, when out of nowhere she tells me that one of her friends, Christine or Christa or something like that, spotted my dad, a.k.a V, a.k.a ChansDad, a.k.a Venkatesh Venkatesh, a.k.a IndianDad76 leering at her from the balcony of our flat during one of Sandra's yoga sessions.

'Anyway, Irene is Christa's friend and enrolled a few months ago. And she's the one who told me about all those orphans and how we should invest in her startup that finds them loving parents. Parents who live in nice condos on Venice Beach.'

'What do you mean leering?' I ask, but Sandra either doesn't hear me over DJ Morf's classic hit from the summer of '23 that's been on repeat for what seems to be at least the last hour while he's nipped to the loo (or getting blown in the pantry by one of the waiters) or she decides to ignore me while sucking up that green goo until it disappears between her pink glossy lips. She stares to our right, past the other tables, past the highway and presumably resting her eyes on the beach.

I follow her gaze and I see Milo, our video guy, perched on a step stool ladder on the fake beach sand, launching instructions through his red megaphone to a hundred, bronze bodies hoping to become immortals on MEEEE. For a full minute, they will bend, flex, stretch and repeat after V: OMMMMMMMM. And then they'll breathe out. Breathe in. And repeat OMMMMMMMM. And then again. Breathe out. Breathe in. And repeat.

V is the face of YoGuys (that's 'guy' pronounced the French way). Sandra is too white. I'm not brown enough. But V, or 'We', as a fresh-off-the-boat Indian would pronounce his name, is perfect. His brown skin is almost black, the Tamil kind of black, which is a shade below the black kind of black. On top of his oval head, that rug of untamed, seaweed-like hair still screams years of abuse and neglect. The day after he reappeared in my life, almost thirty years after I thought I'd got rid of him, the day I had to introduce him to Sandra as my 'dad', he went through two leopard patterned plastic combs (#PingsDollaDollaStore) until we decided to video and post him struggling to tame the tangles just for a laugh. Three years later the #TameThisMofoHair video has raked up almost 5.5m views and is still climbing.

That's the power of V and it was only the beginning for us. We pasted a bindi on his forehead, grew out his beard, threw that sanyasi outfit over him and got him to roll a couple of beads through his fingers. Then at the start of our videos we got him to chant some shit that sounded like Sanskrit. Once he started selling our yoga mats, he went all Yale pronunciation on us.

So, we asked him to fake it. We got him to speedupbigtime-andtalkreallyfastwithoutanyspacesorbreaths. Roll those aarrrrs. Round those V's, V. Exaggerate everything and then exaggerate it again. Do the head roll, V. More, roll it more. Bring out that Indian you. In the end his words sounded like the sound guy was shaking pebbles in an empty can of baked beans.

The whole world believed us. Cultural appropriation 101: if it works, don't sweat it. Besides, no one gives a fuck. Our followers, white, middle class, 25–35-year-old, privileged yuppies certainly don't. They see his brown skin, his fat caterpillar tache, crawling over his dry, sunburnt lips and the money rolls in for classes, yoga mats, incense sticks, heaters for Ashanti yoga, loin cloths, charity for slum dwelling kids in Bombay and anything else V holds for the camera. After that we just made one staged video after another. Hey look! There's V doing a handstand and falling #ClumsyVHandStand - hahahahahaha - 10,000 hits in four hours - Hey there's V learning to drive - Oh my God! Did he just run over a cow? #HolyCowDriver - 15,000 hits in an hour.

And today's video will be the icing on the cake. It will take us into the stratosphere and, in a few days, with the video raking in hits, we'll sign a five-year contract with the biggest footwear producer in the world.

Just one more video, V. And then I can get rid of you.

'I like their idea but I'm not so keen on Irene's look, you know?' Sandra is still speaking. It takes me a few seconds to realise she's back to or never left her monologue on helping the poor in Africa.

'She wears Marie Farah and that was so last year, plus I think her teeth are crooked and her gums show way too much when she stretches that smile and that's no good for the videos.'

'Sandy, what do you mean leering?'

She pries her lips off the straw and says: 'WOT?'

'About V. You said Krista, Kristina saw him leering at her from the balcony. How does she know he was leering?'

Sandra, sneering at me, has an incredulous look on her face. It's not the first time I've zoned out during one of her speeches on equality or poverty. And it's not the first time I've wondered why I'm still seeing her. Oh, I forgot. The sex, that's why.

'First of all, it was Chrissy. And that's with a KAY and one ES. Not a SEE and two ESSESS. K-R-I-S-Y, Maurice's little thing on the side? Remember? The one who got that second-rate nose job and it melted.'

I motion her to get on with it.

Sandra lets out an exasperated breath and it sounds like she's been keeping it in for a while. 'Listen Chan, she's sure he was leeeeering because that's what you'd expect from a seventy something with an unfiltered bird's eye view of hard bodies flexing, bending and sweating it out in Spandex. I mean, she was upside down but it's difficult to miss a bloke drooling over you, while you stretch, spread your thighs and giggle, during a whole forty-five-minute routine. It's creepy.'

I'm thinking of Krisy-with-a-KAY-and-one-ES upside down when Sandra quips: 'Not to mention he had a visible hard-on.'

'A hard-on? Jesus Sandra, it's V we're talking about. It's thanks to him we're raking it in, you know? Anyway, what do you mean, upside down?'

'Oh. We were doing downward dog.'

154

'So, she couldn't have seen him then.'

She raises her left brow.

'Come on, there's just no way you spot that kind of detail upside down.'

And before I can take it back and just accept it for what it is, Sandra swipes the napkins, cutlery, and our green juices to one side of the smooth, black stone marble table, climbs up on her hands and knees, and moulds herself into the shape of a pyramid, with her bum pointing upwards. Behind her, and framed in her pyramid, several customers have turned round and are approaching us to selfie this moment. With her head turned towards them, I imagine she's winking or giving them her signature orgasmic look with her mouth in the shape of an 'O'. The same one she threw me years ago when we first met, each of us with only a thousand followers and an insatiable hunger to swallow more.

'Now let's see,' she mutters as she stretches in her Lycra pants and yoga tank top by LolaOrange, for whom she's an ambassador (but is about to switch to AthKeta because the BBC uncovered '200 BANGLADESHI EMPLOYEES ON $2 A DAY MAKING $400 SIGNATURE YOGA PANTS FOR THE HADIDS' #StopCheapLabour #DontBuyLolaOrange, besides AthKeta are paying her an extra cool mil). She swivels her head which sits now on her chestnut-coloured wavy hair like a meatball on a mountain of spaghetti and then, while still in Downward Dog, she continues her defence of Krisy. 'Now you see Chan,' she says, 'I can clearly see what's happening over there.'

Between us and the beach is a six-lane behemoth made of

concrete, that runs from Santa Fe all the way to Minnesota, shielded by rusty, fluorescent barriers on either side. A black sedan with tinted windows comes to a sudden stop in the middle of the highway; the car directly behind it swerves past and its driver leaves a barrage of spittle and abuse hanging in the air. The driver of the black sedan, wearing a matching black tie, steps out and opens the passenger door. A black stocking clad leg appears and then, for what seems like an agonising minute, it moves aside to make way for another.

Meanwhile cars scream past, but the driver and legs remain rooted to the spot. I notice that all eyes in the bar are on this scene, Sandra, still in downward dog is utterly forgotten and, when a car tugging a boat crawls past blocking the view for almost ten seconds, people contort themselves into absurd angles, tilt, stand on tables and hop to catch a glimpse of this person.

When the passenger, a woman with wrap-around shades in a light beige-babydoll outfit finally emerges, no one seems to know who she is. But you can hear mutterings, ideas, wrong ones, pathetic ones and, of course, everyone clicks. You can almost see all the media floating into the clouds to add to Amazon's infinite storage servers.

Various paper bags hang and dangle rather ceremoniously from this woman's hands and arms. Sandra is listing them off like an inventory.

'Givenchy, Mario Llosar, Man, this girl has taste, she looks like Miss7, the one who got a million hits gyrating in front of the pyramids, #pyramidsaresexyagain, anyway those are probably

Jimmy Choos, you know what, I'll just call it, they ARE Choos, but I'm pretty sure those are last year's model.'

The babydoll woman, who could be Miss7, donkey kicks the door shut with her Jimmy Choos, straightens into a scarecrow pose and glides Swan-Lake-style across the road towards us, as more cars scream to a stop, drivers hurl abuse, then tire, simmer and melt in her performance until she's nudged through a gap in the barrier and floated over to the bar next to us, which, like ours, has a terrace crawling with half-naked waiters, though their servers are female.

Following, maybe a foot above her, like a halo, swivels a mini drone camera capturing her every move. Some patrons from our bar break from their reverie and scramble towards her, tripping and falling over each other but keeping their phones aloft and always recording.

'Yup. Definitely Miss7 and those are last year's Jimmy Choos. See? And she's wearing blue eye shadow and a heavy shade of cream which sadly doesn't hide the wart on her...'

'OK, Sandra. OK. Your friend Krisy with a Kay saw it all because she's got amazing eyesight like you. And so, V, who also happens to be my dad,' and here I pause. Because it sounds awkward. My dad. It's just so damn hard to say that - I need to take a breather. Jesus it's so hard to say. 'My dad V, V, V is a perv? So now what?'

'I wouldn't worry about it, Chan. Just get him a RebootTM,' she quips turning her head towards me. She crinkles her nose, squints her eyes, and adds 'but do it before you sign the deal with Slam. Coz, you go there with V looking and acting the way he is right now? All they'll see is a lawsuit walking through the door.'

Watching her as she breaks from her pose, and thinking of her friends in yoga pants, all with impeccable finishes to their jawbones, hips, bums, new implants, upper east side Johnson Heights women, created and honed for social media, stretching, bending, and sweating, I wonder if I'm leering. I wonder if I would have had the same reaction as my dad.

Am I having the same reaction right now?

Am I being filmed?

When will I need a RebootTM?

Everyone's had something done to them. Unless you're born perfect. Which let's admit it right now, you're weren't and may never be. But you can get close. You must have done your lips, that new look from DeeMaggio, fuller lower and upper lips, in line with your symmetrical face courtesy of Symetrix, which, of course is one of the first things you gifted yourself. Or your hair. Or your toes. It's so cheap now it's not even worth asking Why. It's about When and How fast. And since Bangladesh (or was it Myanmar?) began printing flesh, it's just a matter of time before you edge even closer to perfection.

And don't tell me that you're not that kind of person, that you're not vain. Oh, you did it for the burns you sustained after a major car crash? Well, boo-fuckin-hoo. I feel for you, but you did it all the same.

A RebootTM is just one step closer to being completely human. That final step when your brain catches up with the rest of your body. Your mind gets rewired. Literally.

The Head of the Federation had it done to him a year ago and the whole procedure was live cast. Today, they say his memory is sharper than ever, that the decisions he makes are done without doubt or lag. A month ago, he finally cluster bombed a city in the north of some Arab country - it was something his generals had been deliberating for the last decade. Who cares if it was the right or wrong decision? Point is a decision was made quickly.

So, are we any closer to world peace? I hear you asking. No, but the reboot surgeons hit pay dirt. Queues began appearing all over the country for reboots. People began lining up their parents and grandparents for reboots.

I'm walking towards V, who's sitting on the beach staring out to sea, and I'm preparing a speech, ripping it apart, starting again, but really wishing this would just go away, while, in the meantime, I'm trying not to trip over myself, my feet sinking and twisting in this sand, that's not really sand but some pulverised wood or sawdust brought in from West Africa that's been here so long I can't remember what was here before. Walking towards me, I see Milo, our video guy, who is still holding his megaphone, a few feet from me. He stops, turns around in the direction of the yoga models, shouts out something about stretching the five-minute break to ten, and I think, Oh shit, now what?

As it turns out, there's more bad news although, in retrospect, not as bad as the breaking news of V sporting a hard-on while watching yoga. But it's bad enough for me to accept that this won't go away. Not without some kind of work done to his head.

When I finally get rid of Milo, reassuring him, wearing my optimist mask, that we won't run over budget, I'm back to where I started, looking for words, as I stand in front of V, who is sitting cross legged on the sand, in his orange sanyasi outfit, personally tailored using the latest VR tech by a designer who lives in Lapland, more famous for her flexibility during her online Pilates sessions than her knowledge on Indian spirituality. We sent her a photo of what a sage should look like, and she printed it.

V has his eyes closed, his arms lay resting on his knees, beads run through the fingers of his right hand.

'V.'

His body shows only the slightest movement of shallow breathing. I wonder whether this is real. His meditation, his godliness, because as far as I know it's supposed to be fake. And the only ones who think it's real are our ten million plus subscribers.

'V, we need to talk.'

When he opens his eyes, it's a slow paced, muscle-by-tiny-muscle process, the kind of thing that would surely test even a monk's patience.

'Chandrasekhar!' he is beaming.

He's the only one who calls me that. Well, my mum did, when she was alive.

'What's hanging?'

'Milo says you've been making multiple trips to the loo.'

His expression doesn't change, and if there was any sun, the light reflected off his shiny whites would blind me.

'Everything ok with you?'

'Why not?' he says, curling his hand in the air, like he's squeezing a tennis ball, a classic V move, first seen on Episode 35 of the V chronicles: The 99 Ways of V. 'A man has to go when a man has to go, bacha.'

I release myself from his penetrating eyes and scan around to find something else interesting. Some of the models have begun to make their way back, Milo is climbing onto his ladder.

'But four times in an hour?' I ask without looking at him, my words settling into the stifling hot air around us. 'We're bleeding cash every minute with these girls, every time they undulate or bend over, I lose a hundred, and there's a hundred of them, so you can do the math. Also, he says you've been annoying some of the girls.'

'I'm not so sure Milo is the guy, Chandrasekhar. His Bollywood style is not so Bolly, it's more just the wood, catch my drift.' He says this and laughs. It's standup. He thinks he's in a standup club.

'Well, maybe you should have thought about that before you punched Tarek.' Tarek, Milo's predecessor, who we hired to do the breakdance video.

'That fool didn't even know what breakdance means! What a fool! But I know, I was there in the eighties not you not anybody I was giving him a much-needed history lesson.'

'You broke his front teeth! How many history teachers have done that to you? You're lucky he didn't sue. Mind you, that would have certainly broken the internet.'

'You see that's the thing with you Chandu. Everything is about these silly videos and the internet. Is this all you care about?'

'Yes, and you're living off it. And if we do this one more video, just one more video, we don't need to worry any longer.'

'But I don't need, WE don't need any more money Chandu my boy!'

'Sandra says you've been acting kinda strange, that you haven't been yourself lately and that maybe you need to get yourself checked out, maybe we should fix you up, get you a RebootTM.'

He's up on his feet, looking straight at me, wagging his finger in my face. V only comes up to my shoulder so he has look up at me by tilting his head considerably, it must look funny to the onlooker. In this case, Milo and a hundred, bored, yoga models.

'No reboot. No.' He begins pacing, his feet disappearing into the sand and at one point I think he's going to sink knee deep. 'No. No. No. Definitely No. It is not human,' and here he pauses, for what, dramatic effect? I don't know.

'Did you see what they did to that boy's mum?' he's speaking, walking around in circles.

'What boy? What mum?'

'That one, Maximus something or other.'

'What? Marcus, Marcus's mum?'

'Yes, yes, that's the one. Don't try and act like it was all good, they took her and did a number on her and now she's crazy.'

Well, that's not entirely wrong. Marcus decided or was coerced by his girl to get his mum a reboot. Now, he's not exactly big league like V. An ex-premier league footballer, retired in '24 after some rickshaw rider in Mumbai knocked him down (incidentally, the idiot was looking the wrong way when he stepped off the curb #RickshawDriversHaveRightsToo), tried to get a following selling Fresh Air but when Coca Cola took over he got burnt in their marketing path; and now has a few hundred K stragglers, probably subscribers who've been dead for over a year. And that was the problem. With little or no following, a handful of cash and not much influence, he decided to get his mum a reboot-sans-safety-insurance-guarantee from Doctor Magoo, your friendly neighbourhood drugstore pharmacist, for dirt cheap.

And he videoed it. It's not much of a video but the results were clear.

BEFORE: mum began to freak out when one of those house cleaning bots spoke to her (100k hits, #oldpeopleRpathetic).

AFTER: mum solves four-digit multiplication problem and calculus in a few minutes (300k hits in a couple of hours, #rebootyourmumnow).

And it would have been fine if he'd left it at that. Except, thinking that this was his comeback moment, he kept filming for the rest of the week. First there was the incident with the dog. Then there was road rage and then the final video before he disappeared was of her walking around the house like a zombie muttering 'Here, Marcus, my little baby boy, come on out Marcus. Mama's here.'

'Not only is it NOT human, it's Inhuman.'

V looks like he's on the verge of tears, but this is surely all an act, my eyes roam the beach, the palm trees, the highway, and I'm

163

doing the numbers and the hits this could bring us. Dramatic by intention or not this has all the makings of a modern-day opera based on the real-life transformation of the world's most famous yogi, starring the yogi himself.

'Listen to me please.'

The sea remains a flat tray serving just the one oil tanker and a man in a wetsuit paddling his extra-large surfboard away from all this. Maybe towards the tanker. To bomb it and film himself while he does it. It wouldn't be the first time.

'Look at me Chandrasekhar! Look at me! Where are you?'

When I do look at him, I see that a tear has burst out and it trickles down his cheek. 'It's like a lobotomy, do you know what that is like? They used to do that,' he faces me as he says this, his eyes scrunched up, incredulous. 'Do you? They tried to do it to your mother, poor, poor …'

'This isn't about her; this is about your behaviour which is becoming increasingly inappropriate.'

'What have I done? Mmm? What?'

'Well.' I hadn't prepared for this and now I find myself without the evidence ready to back it up. 'Well. How about that thing with the Marsens? You lost it there. They've been our, my neighbours for decades.'

'Oh, come on she deserved that, that stupid, stupid. She's racist, and you know it.'

'Yeah. Maybe. Maybe. But she recorded it. You know? And they record everything, you know that. Anyway, ok, forget that. How about that thing with Mr Mahmood, going around pissing in his bushes, cutting them up.'

'Ah,' he waves his hand through the air, 'also racist.'

'He's a Pakistani!'

'That doesn't mean he can't be racist.'

'Whatever. It doesn't mean you can piss in or cut penis shapes into his animal topiary. Hey, stop walking away from me.'

And like an apology, he returns, words running out of his mouth at that speed, that speed we got him to master '#Isthisallyoucareabouthuh? Videos, hits, followers.'

'Don't do that, don't try the guilt thing on me, besides, if that's what this is about, I can pay you back,' I press my finger into his chest, 'with interest.'

He looks dumbfounded for a second. Like what does he think? I don't need to be in debt to him.

He grabs my hand and I feel queasy. 'Of course, it's not about that Chandu. When your mum and I sent you abroad to study, we did so with all our heart, of course we weren't expecting anything in return but, but you're throwing it away.'

'And you're living off it by the way. You know where the exit is, you can go, leave anytime.'

V looks stunned and he's sinking into the sand. Or is it that I feel taller as I speak. I continue and even though there is something deep in me trying to stop me, something else has gotten hold of my tongue, and my jaws and mouth, and the words just appear before me, and I can't stop.

'In fact, leaving might be the cheaper and best option considering what happened at the yoga class yesterday.'

He opens his mouth, but nothing comes out and he closes it again. His eyes are looking through me to the sea behind us.

'Yeah, that's just sick.' I pause, and for effect, add, 'Dad.'

After what seems like an hour, he turns and trudges away towards the highway and I remember a poorly edited video that showed a woman walking into traffic on a six-lane highway, just like this one, and getting rammed by a truck and trailer. She rolled, and rolled, and rolled under every single pair of wheels until the truck finally skidded to a complete stop. I'd seen that video for the first time when I was ten, at school during recess, on someone else's phone. And when I went home, that day, after school, I had watched it over and over again on my mum's laptop.

I'm on my way, in my beat-up Nissan 4000, to Curzon Heights where I expect to find V. Since our conversation earlier this morning, he's been gone, and the filming cancelled. We paid the yoga girls and promised to be in touch soon. Technical difficulties, Milo told them, in his best positive voice.

I live in one of those new development blocks, a hundred percent green, all amenities within the actual compound, several round-the-clock top of the range bot-guards and four infinity pools on the rooftop. V's been sharing my apartment with me since he broke his hip, while trying to climb out of a bathroom window. He claims he was stuck. After that it was too risky to let him live on his own, Sandra and I had a lot riding on him.

I have to take Interstate 40 today because some half-wit bot flew an aerotaxi into a Cesna plane, bringing them both down into my usual route, causing a massive fire, spawning a video, that went viral, of a burning man and bot running around in circles and diverting everyone outside city limits. The motorway I'm on is an ugly, chunk of concrete that's been festering as long as V, perhaps longer, and can't be taken down because a tribe has been burying their dead between pillars for the last twenty odd years, making it a #SacredHighway. As I drive over these dead bodies, half a mile ahead, floating over the motorway, between two exit signs, is a hundred-foot white woman with a bright pixelated smile who is supposed to look like she's come out of a cardio workout, a white towel hanging around her neck. She hovers upright with her hands on her hips next to the words: GET YOUR MUM HER REBOOT TODAY. SHE DESERVES IT. As I get closer and I crane my neck to get a better look, I see that during this month (and this month only) they will throw in a new pair of hips or shoulders or eyes. But there's small print. There's always small print, even on something this big and anyway, I can't make it out because by then I've gone past her. In the rear-view mirror I notice the same advert but bizarrely it's her back that I see and instead of hips and shoulders, it's an offer for new glutes.

When I arrive, I know V isn't home because it doesn't smell of incense, which even though he knows I find appalling, he lights every day, convinced that these musky smells will rouse my interest in our ancestors (some of whom are probably buried under that highway, although in fact they were a different kind of Indian).

I grab a chilled 100% alcohol Heineken #IfItTastesLikeAlcoItIsAlco from the fridge and as I swing the door

167

shut one of V's paper photos slips off and glides through the air until it lands face up on the mahogany floorboards next to my Balenciagas on which I spent a cool grand. A man pushes a chubby boy on a plastic motorbike, through a park covered in red and orange leaves, while in the background a white woman, wearing a salwar kameez, watches on.

When he moved in a year ago, the only thing he carried with him, apart from a set of old clothes, was this photo, the same one he showed me when he came back into my life almost five years ago.

Before placing it on the fridge, he stood there studying it, rubbing his fingers along the edges, caressing mum, and me, as if, if he did it hard enough, we would come alive and give him a massive hug, forgiving him for leaving us to fend for ourselves. Without taking his eyes off the photo, he said, 'She loved that dress, that pink and green, with lines and flowers. She never wanted to change, be like the others. Her hips were wider. Her feet bigger. Her nose like a hook. But she loved herself like that.' Or it was something along those lines. And then he placed it on the barren fridge, like it had always belonged there.

Now, every time he grabs a drink, he reminds me that I've got her eyes, golden hair and looks, but insists that I have his brains. Charming. V says a lot of things. V makes fake videos. And now V leers at women in yoga pants.

I walk up to his room and swing the door, which is ajar, wide open, banging it into the small bedside table, the only purchase he's made in the last year. Above it, hanging on the wall from a drawing pin, is a black framed poster of a group called Public Enemy, which apart from the Golden Suit he wore to the cancelled breakdance video is the only other decoration. The mattress, which has no cot (because Chandu, it's better for my back. You should try it!) is leaning up against the wall, and where it should be, is a mat, the kind you would normally find in a gym, and one that I've seen him using for his breakdance practice.

When he pitched the breakdance video to me, he had told me how huge it was during his time. It came from the Bronx, he'd said.

'The Bronx! Chandrasekhar, the Bronx! It will make a comeback, mark my words Chandrasekhar, mark my words!'

This was a few weeks after his little accident. An accident that cost me:

New hip, top of the range. $10000

New shoulder, mid-range. $6750

Anti-slip sole implants. $1000 x 2

Surgery costs. $5000 (minus a thirty percent discount because while I was live streaming the surgery, the surgeon pulled his mask down, winked and now has several new clients).

I sit on the mat staring at that suit, imagining that the bulb hanging from the ceiling is reflecting golden light all over me, and I'm wondering where he could be, if he really did leave and I feel, I don't know, sorry? No, I decide without much thought. Not sorry.

'I'll get this contract signed, with or without you,' I say to the golden suit hanging on the wall.

Maybe I'll add a clause about V. Maybe I'll find another fake dad. More real than V could ever be.

When I finish the beer, I chuck it into the corner of his room, reach for his music box thingy which he calls a boombox and I push down on the play button. There's a hiss and crackle, and then some ancient rap music blasts out the speakers and I let myself fall back down on the floor, on the mat, and I stare up at the ceiling, at a ventilator fan and its three wooden blades, that he salvaged from a dump along with the boombox, his Sony Walkman, Airs, and other brands I'd never heard of.

From my hip pocket, I pull out my glasses, unfold and put them on. A display appears above me and I ask for biological problems in the elderly, and when the only things that come up are Reboots, robot arms, hips, hands and entirely new memories, I ask for a summary of results all the way back to the 1990s. I can feel the AI thinking, cranking and then finally it lists a summary on retirement, stress, poor quality of life, dementia and Alzheimer's. The most recent video dates from 2025 and it feels as though I've stumbled onto a topic that's long forgotten - there's little or no interest in the forums. The holograms swirling above me show old people, their experiences with loved ones, the discomfort and embarrassment it caused. I read about a group of elderly people in the 21st century, who were sent off to a distant island as an experiment to isolate them (or just get rid of them.) Deviant sexual behaviour was also a clear sign of a problem. Sandra and her friends in spandex flash across my thoughts. Reading my mind, the pages automatically open to yoga poses, videos showing stretches, sweat, more alluring positions and before I can flip the sense or force myself to step away, sexual and rampant behaviour fill the air, and women in yoga pants two sizes too small for them undulate around me to some funky beat, and soon there is no more yoga, pants or music, just the sound of moaning and grunting.

After I've come, I feel tired and ashamed, or maybe just ashamed. Amidst this, a realisation dawns, maybe V isn't losing his mind; he's simply driven by desire. Can octogenarians even feel desire? Opting not to go down that route, I contemplate going to my own room, my bed #Vividus #FerrisRafauli, an opulent, handcrafted creation. It was V's gesture to mark our five-millionth follower.

He had remarked, 'Craftsmanship is a dying art, Chandrasekhar. See, this bed. It is hand made. It took over six hundred hours to build. Everything moves too swiftly now. One blink, and it's vanished! Rest is paramount, my son. You need sleep, there's too much chaos, too many connections. Too much wiring everywhere. You're too wired, my son. Sleep.'

'Sleep.'

When I open my eyes I'm in a park, its autumn and I'm looking up at someone who looks like V, except he has only a face, three arms and he's spinning and it takes me another minute to realise it's the fan in V's room and once I switch off his boombox thingy, which is making a squiggly sound akin to people shouting underwater, that it dawns on me that the apartment is completely silent and that this can only mean one thing, V isn't and probably hasn't been home since yesterday.

The sky is a bowl of sludgy, grey soup that drips over the concrete landscape. As I exit the city, there is a light drizzle, and everything around me, buildings, cars, people, are a blur and my brain, working like a pair of goggles transmitting gigabits of information over a copper wire that can only be used for snail mail, feels slow, disoriented, and painful.

The overpass again. Cleared of debris, the bot, and the charred remains of the human involved in last night's crash. I take the exit to the bot graveyard, about two miles out from the city. It used to be the biggest in the country until the rains washed about five hundred odd bots into the city and every street corner was strewn with bots of all shapes and sizes, in different states of decay.

I remember V being distraught that day. It was like he'd seen dead children littering the street, not bots and when I'd told him they were just chunks of metal he had given me that look. The same one he did yesterday when the reboot came up.

Since then, he would visit what was left of the graveyard without fail every Saturday, the only day we didn't have such a heavy schedule and sometimes he'd be there almost three or four hours. I once came back from a night out at Silvia's or was it Area53, I don't know, at 3 in the morning and found his room empty. Later, I woke to the smell of burning and ran downstairs expecting to find the lounge on fire, only to be met with the sight of V waving a tea towel over a contraption called SMEG. A toaster. That toasts bread. Bread for fucks sake. Who even eats that shit now?

And like that, every weekend the flat would accumulate something retro: a tiny fridge that he called his mini-bar, although he didn't touch alcohol; a camera that made instant photos but needed special paper which no longer existed, so it just went into a display case, a spider-like bot that cleaned sinks; an old television, which like the fridge was just empty.

When I arrive, I leave the car near the north most entrance and grab an umbrella from the glovebox. After walking half a mile in several directions, it was no surprise to find him, sitting on the rim of a bathtub in the middle of one of the debris under an overpass, poking with a screwdriver, at what looks like a robot waitress.

He must have heard me coming because without looking up, he says, 'You know what this is? This is a Honda Waiting Bot. I haven't seen one of these in almost three decades. It was one of the first ones I used to assemble that rolled off the factory line. You were only, well it was a very long time ago.'

'You slept here last night?' I ask, knowing full well he had. I could see his little Fiat parked beside a forklift.

'She was standing in here,' he says pointing at the bathtub, 'hiding behind the shower curtain.' A curtain emblazoned with a colourful picture of Jesus and the caption - I saw that. The bot, which had its front casing open, and its copper entrails spilling out, was a female one, with large blue eyes, a round face and black hair tied firmly behind her head. She was still wearing a tux and holding onto a dinner tray covered with the remnants of what looked like green pea soup.

'First, I decided not to. It's been so long since I healed them.' He shuts the front lid and begins wiping his patient down with a cloth, focusing all his attention on a stain near the hip. The drizzle which is becoming heavier helps. 'What do I know now? Today's programmers are a different breed, and their creations are almost like us.'

The stain is beginning to fade, at least it seems so in this light or is it my imagination because, perhaps, watching him scrub so hard I want it to disappear.

'Then, while sitting in the car, I thought. Why not?' He stands up, smoothing some strands of her hair off her face, sliding them behind her ear. 'What will happen if no one takes care of her?' He reaches round her neck and fiddles with something. 'Nobody wants them any longer - they are so outdated.' There is a whizzing sound. 'But that doesn't mean they are useless, no?'

The bot begins to make buzzing and whirring sounds, not too loud but loud enough to stir some movement amongst the debris.

'It doesn't mean they should be forgotten. They deserve better.'

A few meters away, a bird hops onto a sofa, and chirps. It's a rather sharp, out of tune, sound. And shrill. It stops as abruptly as it began.

'Good morning Mr. Singred,' says the Honda bot, moving its lips like a human. 'How about that medication, sir?'

I take a few steps closer. Neither its eyes nor voice are very lifelike. Things have improved over the last twenty, thirty years.

'See,' says V, finally looking at me, his arm around the bot, and with a smile that spreads across his face. 'There's still life here.' He waves at the debris around him. The bird, I see, has remained frozen to its spot on the sofa.

'With a little help, she's good as new, we can take her home and she can...'

174

'Sorry, that does not compute,' the bot cackles.

V continues, 'She can do some housework and serve ...'

'Sorry, that does not compute.' she repeats. And again. And again. And again.

V pokes behind her neck but the bot keeps repeating the same thing, this time in a sharper, higher tone, reminding me of someone.

'SorrythatdoesnotcomputeSorrythatdoesnotcomputeSorrythatdoe snotcomputeSorrythatdoesnotcompute.'

V is now stabbing at her neck with his thumb like he's stuck in an elevator that refuses to move.

'Well almost,' he says trying to laugh, 'almost as good as new.' He picks up the screwdriver that lay by his feet and rams it into her neck, digging it into her, twisting his arm, twisting, twisting until, I can see he's tired.

But she just won't stop nagging.

'I don't know what's wrong. I don't know. She looked fine. I fixed her.' He steps back from the bot. He looks at me, his eyes red, dug deep into his skull, surrounded by black rings. His face haggard, his hair, for a change, clean, straight, wet. He puts his hands in his pocket and looks down at his feet.

And then, as if in slow motion, he lifts something from the bathtub and when he straightens up, he swings it at her head. It's a hammer. The kind you employ when there's nothing left to repair. It lands across her cheek, and sparks fly from her left eye. For a moment I feel like she's blindsided, the same way I am, she doesn't know what hit her. She doesn't scream and if there's a reaction, it goes unnoticed between the first blow and what comes next. V swings again. The hammer sails into her chin and then her forehead. Her head swivels.

The bot, however, persists in her ceaseless chatter. So, V swings again and this time the blows begin to rain down on her mercilessly and unyielding. The back of her head, across the right side of her face, which until now had remained unblemished, and frozen with half a smile. Her neck, the crown of her skull. The hammer snags momentarily and V exerts some effort to dislodge it and then he goes for her eyes, nose, jugular.

In the end, her head topples and hangs, from red, green and blue wires, trailing down her back. And still, there's a sound, milder than before but it's audible, nevertheless.

The bird tweets again.

'Sorry. Compute. Sorry. Compute.'

V breaks open the front case with the screwdriver and yanks out her entrails, and then, only then, with one last, muffled 'Sorry', does it stop.

He lets go of the hammer which hits the tub with a clunk, and then shoves his hands back into his pockets and stands staring at his feet. Wet, and covered in mud.

Somewhere another bird is chirping but I can't tell if it is real or a bot.

Watch closely.

I'm sat with V in Slam's head office car park. That's us in the beat-up Nissan among the Ferraris and Maserati's. I'll have one, maybe even two of those, when this works out.

I hunch over the wheel, peer through the windscreen and drink in the famous logo standing proudly on the roof, taking up half the skyline. It looks like it has sliced open the sky and made it bleed red, orange, and purple.

The red, blue, and green neon lights from the big shoe sign and the LCD display wash over us and my stone-cold co-pilot, V, who sits staring out the window. A new, rebooted V. More efficient. Faster. More intelligent and more clinical in his approach to the business.

A few days ago, we wrapped up filming for the beach video. In the action scene, while the hundred models 'OM'-ed, breathed in and out, a young blonde woman surfing the waves comes into focus. She's a pro-surfer but for this video she plays an amateur who falls off the board and is caught in a whirlpool. Splashing and gasping for air, shouting for help, she begins to drown. Cut to V, who is sitting cross legged, in his orange sanyasi outfit, rolling black beads between his fingers. His moustache twitches, a classic V signal (first seen in Episode 42 of the V chronicles: The Caterpillar and his Apprentice) that trouble is afoot. He bounces to his feet, spins toward the sea where the helpless surfer is being engulfed by the waves. V kicks through wave after wave, tames the whirlpool, saves the girl and her surfboard too, the brand painted across it in red, white, and blue, is the last frame we see.

Today, #YogiToTheRescue is the most watched video on the planet, with almost a billion hits and counting.

'We made it V. We made it. We're the biggest thing on the planet,' I say, turning to him and placing my hand on his shoulder.

'We need to listen to their offer and then walk away,' V says in his Yale accent, shrugging my hand off. 'Then we come back in and talk about the exclusivity clause. And when they come back with another offer, we leave again.'

I open my mouth to say something, but he raises his hand.

'We need to get them to value our creativity. So, we ask for a wider exclusivity window. And then after coming back in again, we add a performance bonus tied to engagement metrics.'

He reaches over to straighten my tie and pulls out a comb from his jacket which he hands me.

'Finally, we need to put our foot down regarding content ownership, and ensure we retain rights for personal use.'

And then I see it. Something else. Someone else. Not V the 70-year-old star. Not V my so-called dad. Not the homeless guy who, before anyone knew him, before he became V the famous Indian star, darling of social media, before he assumed his role as father of Chan, turned up at my doorstep years ago, with a photo of a kid on a plastic motorbike in his hand. Not that V. This is something else altogether.

'I'll do the talking – in fact – if you like you can stay back in the lobby,' he says without looking at me. 'And when it's all done, we're going to fix you up. And get you a RebootTM.'

Like a jump cut we're in the lobby of the office with its jungle and conservatory like appearance. On the walls, behind the creepers and vines hide footballers and basketball players, frozen in mid sprint or jump, showing off their kit and footwear. The logo gleams, pulses, its alive.

There's a girl with blonde pig tails behind the reception who looks like she's come straight from school to do this job for extra credits and she's hard at work chewing gum. She doesn't take our names because she's seen our video and she, like the other ninety-nine million on this planet, recognises V.

'Who are these guys?' I ask her as she does our visitor passes. I'm looking at one person, the only black guy in the room, like I should know him, like I should have paid attention when I was four or five. He's doing an imaginary slam dunk. There's no hoop, nor ball. I think I hear V snicker, and from the corner of my eye, I see him shake his head but when I look up, he's back to playing the part. Rolling his head and smiling at the girl, who's clipping a red loop onto each of the white, glossy looking visitor passes. 'I have no idea. I just work here,' she says without looking up.

Right after snapping a photo of her with her arms around V's neck, she says to me, 'Hey,' and nodding in the direction of one of the posters, 'I reckon they're all famous.' She slides the cards across the smooth emerald-like surface of the desk and digs out the gum in her mouth. Turning it round in her fingers and studying it carefully, she adds, 'At least, they used to be.'

When I turn back to V, his visitor tag in hand, mine round my neck, he's bro-hugging a slicked-back hair, blond, blue-eyed, all-knowing, all-seeing, Suit and Tie, who immediately launches into consumer market statistics.

'V,' he says in a voice that booms across the lobby, 'you're the A-Bomb.' His hands are around his shoulders. 'You're going to be one of these guys.' He waves his arms and twirls on his heels, like it's all his property, all these people, all these stars. But hey, maybe they are.

'Come on, all you've got to do is sign on the dotted line.' And here this head honcho notices me and says, with his fingers laced with gold rings, gracing V's wrinkly neck 'V, why don't you and your associate here, follow me upstairs.'

'My associate shall remain in the lobby,' V replies without a beat and then as he reaches for his visitor card that hangs off my fingers, he adds, 'There's no need to drag things out.'

'Yo bro forget that card,' bellows Suit and Tie, waving at the visitor card like its filth. 'You're almost family now V and you know V is for visitor?' They laugh and I want to join in but just then Suit and Tie snaps his fingers at the receptionist. 'Jean honey, keep this young fella entertained while we're doing business, will you?'

And with that he swivels V around and they shimmy towards the glass elevator.

I watch them walk away, arms linked, like a two-man tango, until they enter the elevator and spin round together. Laughing - Hahaha.

I turn to Jean and hand her V's card. I leave mine on, though it now feels tight and heavy.

'So,' says Jean, who's chewing gum again, maybe a new piece, but more likely the one she'd stored under her desk when we arrived, running her fingers through her hair, with a glint in her eyes she asks, 'must be pretty amazing being his PA, huh?'

But I'm already back to watching V aka VenkateshVenkatesh aka IndianDad76 aka Dad aka SocialMediaGod in the elevator, floating up into the heavens, and I can see the Suit and Tie yakking away, and V nodding and shaking his head, all while looking down at me, and I'm trying to read the expression on his face, but I can't put my finger on it because it's one I don't recognize, or it's an old look in a new format, and I suddenly feel sick, but excited as well because that look will bag new followers, and that means more money but then I feel like throwing up and I don't know why #HappySickFeeling.

But wait. This is all fake anyway, right?